ONLY LOVE

Iola told herself she was being ridiculous to love this man whose world was filled with royalty, luxury, beautiful women. Should she run away before she made things even worse? Tears ran down her cheeks.

"Stop crying, my darling," Sir Wolfe implored.

"Wh . . . what did you . . . say?" she whispered shyly.

"Whoever you may be," Sir Wolfe murmured, turning her face to his, "whatever you have done or whatever you are hiding . . ."

At last his lips were on hers. They seemed to ignite her whole body, taking into his keeping her heart, her soul, everything that was hers and making it a part of himself.

Struggling for words, for breath, she confessed, "No one has ever . . . tried to kiss me . . . until now!"

Bantam Books by Barbara Cartland
Ask your bookseller for the books you have missed

6 The Bored Bridegroom
20 The Flame is Love
46 The Incredible Honeymoon
69 The Dragon and the Pearl
73 The Naked Battle
76 The Castle Made for Love
78 The Saint and the Sinner
79 A Fugitive from Love
80 The Twists and Turns of Love
81 The Problems of Love
82 Love Leaves at Midnight
83 Magic or Mirage
92 The Race for Love
98 The Drums of Love
99 Alone in Paris
100 The Prince and the Pekingese
101 The Serpent of Satan
102 The Treasure is Love
103 Light of the Moon
104 The Prisoner of Love
105 Flowers for the God of Love
106 A Voice in the Dark
108 Love Climbs In
109 A Nightingale Sang
110 Terror in the Sun
111 Who Can Deny Love?
112 Love Has His Way
113 The Explosion of Love
114 Only Love
115 Women Have Hearts

Barbara Cartland's Library of Love series

Ramazan the Rajah
The Money Moon
The Rocks of Valpre

Books of Love and Revelation

The Treasure of Ho

Other Books by Barbara Cartland

I Seek the Miraculous

Only Love

Barbara Cartland

ONLY LOVE

A Bantam Book / January 1980

ISBN 0-553-13392-6

Published simultaneously in the United States and Canada

Bantam Books are published by Bantam Books, Inc. Its trademark, consisting of the words "Bantam Books" and the portrayal of a bantam, is Registered in U.S. Patent and Trademark Office and in other countries. Marca Registrada. Bantam Books, Inc., 666 Fifth Avenue, New York, New York 10019.

PRINTED IN THE UNITED STATES OF AMERICA

DESIGNED BY MIERRE

Author's Note

The word "Kidnapping" is a compound of two slang words—"kid," meaning a child, and "nap" or "nab," meaning to snatch or to seize. The word was originally coined in 1680 to describe the then-prevalent practice of stealing children and sending them to servitude on British plantations in America.

Kidnappers, with the growth of organised crime in the United States during Prohibition, were offered all the rewards of bank robbery with few of the risks.

In the late 1920s it became commonplace for wealthy persons or their children to be "snatched" and held for ransom.

Chapter One

1903

"I have something to tell you, Iola," the General said.

He spoke in his well-articulated voice that could be heard across any Barrack Square.

"Yes, Papa?"

Iola looked up from her plate on which were several slices of under-done beef.

It was the General's favourite dish and every time they had it she thought that she would like the beef to be cooked more and not to have such a large helping.

But as her father carved she found it politic to take what he gave her and not to argue about it.

"I must say," the General continued, "that I am extremely gratified and in a way surprised, but then you are my daughter so it might be expected that you would make a good match."

Iola stared at him in surprise.

"What are you saying, Papa?" she asked in a puzzled tone.

"I am informing you," the General said, "that Lord Stoneham has asked if he can pay his addresses to you and naturally I have given my consent."

Iola stiffened until her whole body was rigid and it seemed for a moment that she had completely lost her voice and the power to think.

Lord Stoneham! Surely her father could not mean the Lord Lieutenant who had called this morning and been closeted with the General in his Study for so long that Aunt Margaret had wondered if they should invite him to luncheon?

But eventually he had left, driving away in his carriage with his crest emblazoned on the panels and his servants wearing his smart livery of Royal blue and orange.

"What did Lord Stoneham want with you, Alexander?" Margaret Herne had asked her brother when he came into the Drawing-Room.

"I will tell you later," the General had replied in a repressive tone. "Luncheon should be ready by now and you know I like my meals on time."

"Yes, of course, Alexander," his sister had said meekly.

They proceeded in to luncheon, the General going first with an air of urgency about him.

Iola had not been curious as her aunt was about Lord Stoncham's visit.

He often called at the Manor to see her father on matters that concerned the County; the General, to his intense gratification, had been appointed Deputy Lieutenant and was only too pleased to represent Lord Stoneham at any function which he was unable to attend himself.

Now she felt that she could not have heard correctly what her father had said to her.

At last, as if her voice came from very far away, she managed to say:

"Did I . . . hear you . . . right, Papa? Are you . . . s-saying that Lord Stoneham wishes to . . . marry me?"

"That is correct!" the General boomed. "He wishes to marry you and in fact is in a hurry to do so."

"B-but ... Papa ... his wife has been dead only for—"

"A year next week," the General interrupted, "and twelve months, as you are well aware, is the prescribed time of mourning."

Aunt Margaret clasped her hands together ecstatically.

"It is the most exciting news I have ever heard!" she cried. "Just think, Iola, you will not only be the wife of the Lord Lieutenant, but you will be able to go to the Opening of Parliament wearing a tiara!"

Her voice seemed almost to tremble with excitement, while Iola, still feeling as if she had turned to stone, said:

"I cannot think, Papa ... why Lord Stoneham should wish to ... marry me. He is ... old ... very old."

"He may be past the first flush of youth, that I grant you," the General replied, "But he is a man I both admire and respect, and he will make you a most commendable husband, there's no doubt about that."

Iola felt herself shudder at the word "husband."

She had never until this moment thought of Lord Stoneham as a man but only as a figure of importance.

She had in fact been gratified when he had danced with her twice at the Hunt Ball which, because he was in mourning, had taken place much later in the year than was usual.

She thought that of course he had singled her out because she was her father's daughter, and she thought the same when he was courteous to her whenever he called at the Manor and when during the last three months she had attended long-drawn-out and very dull dinner-parties that he gave at Stoneham Park.

But never for one second had it struck her that he might be interested in her as a woman, any more than she was interested in him as a man.

"Husband!"

The word seemed to scream at her and echo round the panelled Dining-Room.

"It is a great honour that he has chosen you," the General said as if he spoke to himself. "He will call on you tomorrow at twelve noon, so be ready to receive him."

As he finished speaking he rang the silver bell which stood on the table in front of him and the servants came back into the room.

Iola's plate went away untouched. She refused the pudding and the cheese that followed it, and when her father cut himself a large slice of plum cake to eat while he drank his glass of port, she said in a nervous little voice:

"W-will you . . . excuse me . . . Papa? I do not . . . feel very well."

"Excitement, I suppose," the General remarked. "It's understandable. Run along and lie down. You must look your best tomorrow."

Iola hurried from the room and the General turned to his sister.

"Girls have no stamina nowadays," he complained. "If anything unusual happens they collapse!"

"I expect it has been rather a shock, Alexander," Margaret Herne replied.

"I suppose so," the General admitted. "She has had no other suitors. I thought that young jackanapes Windham was here too often, so I sent him away with a flea in his ear before there was any mischief done."

"I am sure you were right, Alexander. Captain Windham would not have been a suitable *parti* for any daughter of yours."

"That's what I thought. To start with, he is in a bad Regiment."

His sister smiled.

"I am sure dear Iola will see the advantages of

marrying a nobleman of such importance as Lord Stoneham. But of course she is only eighteen, and he is . . ."

"It's not years which count in a man of Stoneham's calibre," the General said. "He has intelligence and a capacity for leadership which is not found amongst the young. Look at the mess that was made of the Boer War! Disgraceful! An exhibition of incompetence I never expected to find in the British Army."

This was a well-worn bone of contention and his sister said hastily:

"As I have said so often, Alexander, they do not make men like you these days, and I am sure Iola will appreciate that she will find many of your qualities in her future husband."

"That's true," the General agreed.

He helped himself to another glass of port and said:

"You had better start thinking about Iola's trousseau. I am prepared to spend a little more than I might have done had her marriage been to a less important man."

His sister smiled with pleasure as she replied:

"You must remember, Alexander, that she will be seen in public as Lord Stoneham's wife, she will be expected to appear with him on public platforms and of course to make her curtsey at Buckingham Palace to the new King."

The General laughed.

"We shall certainly have to spend quite a considerable sum on her gown for that occasion if she's to compete with the elegance of Queen Alexandra. But I expect Stoneham will ante-up once she's his wife!"

He sipped his port before he said, lowering his voice:

"I don't mind telling you in confidence, Margaret,

that he spoke as if he is infatuated with the girl. Between ourselves, I was quite surprised at how eloquent he was about her."

"You mean that he is in love, Alexander?"

"That is not an expression I care for. Far too emotional," the General remarked. "But I suppose I should admit that in this case it appears to be true."

"Then Iola is even luckier than I thought her to be!" Miss Herne exclaimed. "When you said that Lord Stoneham wishes to pay his addresses, it sprang to my mind immediately that the reason he wishes to marry again is that he wants an heir."

"Exactly!" the General said. "It was a great tragedy his boy being killed in Africa. I never thought he would get over it!"

"It is obvious that he has."

"It seems so," the General agreed. "Anyway, he's insistent that the marriage should take place next month, but I didn't say so to Iola in case it should frighten her. I've always understood that girls feel a little nervous and shy about rushing into marriage. Personally, I should have thought a six-month engagement would be more advisable. Give them a chance to get to know each other."

"I remember that you were engaged, Alexander, for nearly a year."

"That's what I was thinking about," the General replied. "But nowadays everything is rush, rush! In my opinion, being too hasty invariably leads to trouble."

"I hope not where dear Iola is concerned."

"No, of course not, but we must do what Stoneham wants."

There was a faint smile on the General's lips as he added:

"We certainly do not want to lose him."

"What a terrible thought!" Margaret Herne exclaimed. "I promise you, Alexander, that I will impress upon Iola how very fortunate she will be to have such a good and important man as her husband."

* * *

The word "husband" was still echoing in Iola's ears as she stood at her bedroom window looking out on the snow-covered ground.

The trees glistening with frost, silhouetted against the wintry sky, made a picture which usually lifted her heart in a manner which she found difficult to put into words.

But now she stared at them blindly and instead saw only Lord Stoneham, feeling that in some detached part of her mind she was examining and analysing him in a way she had never done before.

How could she possibly contemplate for one moment marrying a man who had seemed to her a father-figure?

He was so aloof and lived in a world so different from her own that she thought sacrilegiously that he might be God rather than a human being.

With his white beard shaped in the fashion set by the King, his somewhat portly figure, and his air of consequence, it was not surprising that it had never crossed her mind for one instant that he might be a suitor for her hand.

Because her brothers, who were both much older than she, were now serving abroad she lived a very lonely existence at the Manor.

As a rule she met only the General's elderly friends and the ladies who came to the house to discuss the "good works" to which her aunt was heavily committed, but these guests seldom invited them back.

Even if they did, the General disliked going to most people's houses and invariably refused invitations without consulting either his sister or his daughter.

Therefore, books were Iola's main form of entertainment as well as a means of acquiring knowledge.

The novels of Walter Scott first introduced her to romance and she had followed them with the Classics and a number of sophisticated modern novels like those of Jane Austin and Anthony Trollope.

As she grew up she found herself dreaming of the heroes about whom she had read and also inventing her own.

At the Hunt Ball, which was the first grown-up Ball she had been allowed to attend, she had found it exciting to dance with the younger members of the Hunt in their pink coats.

Although she had been gratified that the Lord Lieutenant had singled her out amongst the other girls, who might all have appreciated such attention, she had thought privately that it was a waste of a dance which she would have enjoyed with a younger man.

But her younger partners had not called on her and they had certainly not approached her father, while Lord Stoneham had.

"He is old, old!" Iola murmured to herself. "Why should he want me?"

She knew that Lady Stoneham had been a large, Junoesque figure who always appeared to be hung with jewels—several rows of large pearls in the daytime and diamonds in the evening, besides a tiara which glittered on her grey hair.

"How could I possibly take her place?" Iola asked herself. "And besides, why should he want me to?"

Then almost as if someone had answered the question aloud, she knew the answer.

Lord Stoneham wanted another son!

The General had been extremely upset when Edwin Stoneham had been killed four years ago.

Iola could remember how Aunt Margaret had wept in sympathy for his bereaved family.

"He was such a charming young man! It seems cruel that he should have been killed, and now there is no heir to the Barony."

"I believe there is a distant cousin," the General had reflected, "but Stoneham has never liked him. It's not a question I care to discuss with him at the moment."

"No, of course not, Alexander!" his sister had cried.

"Damned hard on the fellow, losing his son, but then it's a mistake to have only one, especially when you have an important name to carry on."

The General had spoken with just a touch of satisfaction in his voice.

He had two sons, one in the Army serving with his Regiment in India, the other in Canada, and he was justifiably proud of them.

When Iola had been born her brothers were both more or less grown up; George was at Oxford and Richard was just leaving Eton.

She had often heard her Nanny refer to her as "an afterthought," and for a long time she could not understand what the word meant and had puzzled over it, thinking it meant that there was something wrong with her.

Once she had realised what Iola was worrying about, Nancy had swept away her apprehension.

"Now don't you go worrying your head over the things I say," she had said with a smile. "I talk too much and it's always been my worst fault. My mother's told me that a thousand times."

"What does 'an afterthought' mean, Nanny?"

"It means that your father and mother prayed very hard that they would have a daughter, and then just when your mother thought she was too old, God sent you down from Heaven as a special present for her."

"Did He really, Nanny?"

"Look in the mirror and you'll see for yourself."

"And was Mama pleased?"

"Very, very pleased," Nanny had said, "and so was I, because I could come and look after you."

"And I was the first baby you ever looked after, wasn't I?"

"You were, and I was lucky to get the position. I was afraid I was too young, but your mother took a chance on me, and though I says it as shouldn't, she's never regretted it."

Iola had never regretted it either. She had loved Nanny Dawes more than anybody.

Her mother was beautiful, kind, and loving when she had the time, but she was often away from home, and when she was at home she was too busy to spend time in the Nursery. But Nanny was always there.

Nanny was young enough to run with her in the woods, to play Hide-and-Seek amongst the trees, and to invent stories that there was a dragon lurking in the pine woods, and fairies dancing on the lawn where there were toadstools to show that they had been there.

There were gnomes burrowing underneath the hills and nymphs interwoven with the mists over the ponds and streams, especially first thing in the morning and last thing at night.

Nanny knew all about such fairy-creatures, and it was in fact Nanny who had made Iola aware of men.

"Who was that who said good-morning to us?" she remembered asking when they had passed a smart groom riding up the drive with a note for her father and mother.

"That's Fred," Nanny replied. "He's a handsome fellow and he knows it! He thinks every girl in the County's after him."

"After him for what?" Iola asked.

"Now don't you go asking questions like that. I shouldn't have mentioned it in the first place."

"But I want to know what he is after."

"What all men are after—a pretty girl when he sees one."

"He smiled at you. Does he think you are pretty?"

Nanny tossed her head.

"It's just like his cheek if he did. I knows too much about Master Fred to be taken in by his eloquent eyes and his wily tongue!"

If it was not Fred it was Jim, Clem, or Ben who gave Nanny what Iola had learnt was known as the "Glad Eye," but Nanny would have none of them.

As Iola grew older she became frightened that she might lose Nanny and there was one man named Sid who really worried her.

"You will not marry Sid, will you, Nanny? Promise me! If you do, you will leave me, and I do not know what I would do without you."

"He'd be lucky!" Nanny said enigmatically.

"I do not want him to be lucky," Iola said. "I am lucky to have you, and I love you, Nanny. Promise me, promise me you will not marry Sid!"

Then she learnt that he was in trouble concerning a woman who was working in the house of Lord Hartmakin, who was a friend of the General.

There was a great deal of whispering between Lady Hartmakin and Aunt Margaret.

It was all rather mysterious and Iola gathered that the servant in question had been dismissed without a reference, and Sid had been sacked too.

She thought that for about a week Nanny was rather quiet.

She had a headache which made her cry at night, but to Iola's relief there was no further sign of Sid and after a little while Nanny cheered up and was her usual happy self again.

The most terrible day of Iola's life was when Nanny left.

"She is not to go! I will not let her go!" she had stormed to her mother when she had heard that

Nanny was leaving and her place was to be taken by a Governess.

"She has stayed much longer than I intended in the first place," Mrs. Herne had replied, "but she has taught you quite a lot of your elementary lessons. Now you really must have a proper education. I was quite ashamed when I realised the other day how well the Castleton girl, who is younger than you, can speak French."

"I will learn French! I will learn anything you like if you will let Nanny stay!"

"I am sorry, Iola. You will like the Governess I have chosen for you. She is a very capable woman and your father approves of her too."

"I hate her! I will always hate her because she has made Nanny go away!"

Iola cried and Nanny cried too.

Mrs. Herne found her another position, and Iola said pleadingly on the morning before she went:

"Promise me, Nanny, that you will not love the new children you are going to more than you love me."

"Of course I promise," Nanny answered. "You were my first baby. First babies are very, very special. I could never forget you or stop loving you."

"And I will never love anybody more than you," Iola replied.

Nanny laughed.

"One day you'll get married and have babies of your own, and you'll love them and they'll come first in your life. But always remember that there's plenty of love for everyone—me, them, your father and mother, and lots of other people."

"You are first, you will always be first!" Iola sobbed.

Nanny hugged her, then she said:

"Now don't forget, you promised to write to me, and I'll write to you whenever I get the chance. I shall want to know all you are doing and how much you are learning with the new—Governess."

Just for a moment Nanny's voice broke on the words. Then she had been driven away in the Landau which was kept for the use of the servants, and Iola had rushed up to the Nursery to cry on Nanny's bed until her eyes were too swollen to see out of them.

Nanny kept her promise and wrote to Iola, but her letters got fewer as the years passed.

Iola had written regularly, sometimes long letters, sometimes short, and they had always been written with love.

She thought now that only Nanny would understand what she was feeling. Nanny had always understood as nobody else had ever been able to do.

Her Governesses, and there had been three of them over the years, had been kind and sensible—although only one of them had the gift of teaching—but they had never awakened Iola's imagination as Nanny had been able to do.

"I suppose what I really want in the man I marry is somebody whom I will love in the same way as I love Nanny, but more intensely," Iola said to herself.

She learnt to be analytical when she was alone because nobody else understood.

She was intelligent enough to realise that Nanny had not only awakened her imagination and her idealism, but also in some strange way had made her give the best of which she was capable at the time.

Nobody else had had that ability, and it was something, Iola reasoned, that was a mixture of the intellectual, the physical, and the spiritual.

'It was with Nanny,' she thought, 'that I came alive as a person and could see and feel as I could not do with anybody else.'

As she had grown older she had thought it was

that capacity for living fully that she wanted to find with the man she loved.

Although Nanny had meant so much in her childhood, she sometimes wondered if the influence she had had on her was imaginary and would not be there if they met again.

Two years ago Nanny had written to say that her parents had died and left her their cottage which was in a village only eight miles away from the Manor.

With her employers' permission she was going down for a week to put the cottage in order and shut it up until she would need it on her retirement.

Would it be possible for her to come to the Manor and see her "first baby"?

From the moment Iola had read the letter she was wild with excitement.

It seemed almost too good to be true that she would see Nanny again and talk to her and she would understand as she had always understood.

She could tell her how unhappy she had been at the loss of her mother, how the house seemed empty without her, how difficult her father was at times, and how it could never be the same having Aunt Margaret in her mother's place.

The General had good-humouredly said that the brake could pick up Nanny at the village of Little Waywood and bring her to the Manor.

Unable to wait, Iola had travelled in the brake, tense with excitement and feeling that the horses were moving infuriatingly slowly along the dusty lanes.

Nanny's home was a small thatched cottage at the end of a little village which centred round a Norman Church and an ancient Inn.

Iola thought it was just the sort of village that she had imagined as a background for Nanny, a village which might in fact have come straight out of a fairy-tale book.

When the brake stopped outside Honeysuckle

Cottage, Iola ran down the flagged path to the front door and found Nanny waiting for her.

She looked older—Iola had forgotten that even those we love age—but her smile was the same and her brown eyes were as soft and loving as they had ever been.

"Nanny! Nanny!"

Iola's arms were round her and she was hugging her, and because she was so happy there were tears in her eyes and a break in her voice.

"Now, let me look at you," Nanny said. "Goodness, you've grown into a pretty girl, just as I always knew you would!"

"Oh, Nanny, I have missed you so much! It has never been the same without you. Do you still love me?"

"You know I do. You were my first baby, and a first baby is like a first kiss—it's something one never forgets."

Just for a moment Iola looked surprised and Nanny laughed.

"I remember everything about you," Iola said. "And now that I can see your cottage, I think it is lovely! Just like the one the Gingerbread Witch lived in."

"Fancy you remembering that story!" Nanny said, laughing. "I suppose when I told it to you I was thinking of my home."

It was a small cottage. The front door opened into a flagged kitchen with a rather poky little Sitting-Room behind, which Nanny called "the Parlour," and upstairs there were two bedrooms.

Iola found it enchanting and Nanny showed it to her with pride.

"It belongs to me!" she said. "When I'm too old to go on looking after children, I'll come back here. It's nice to know I've a roof over my head. It's what everybody should have."

"And when you are here, I can come and stay with you . . . that is . . . if you will have me," Iola said.

"You know you'll always be welcome," Nanny replied.

* * *

Iola could hear the voice saying it now, and then she remembered something else.

A letter had come only this morning, but her father's announcement at luncheon had put it out of her head.

Now she drew from the pocket of her gown the envelope addressed to her in Nanny's neat, round, child-like handwriting.

Opening it, she read:

Dear Miss Iola:

You'll be surprised to hear I am leaving here for another job. It's a long story, too long to write about, but I hope I'll have a chance to tell you what's happening. I'll be at Honeysuckle Cottage from next Wednesday 12th 'til the 14th. I'm hoping that you can come over and see me, or I'll have the chance to come to you.

I'm wearing your Christmas present, and nice and warm it is. I hope you're keeping well.

God bless you, and my love,

Nanny

Iola read the letter through twice very carefully, as if it were a talisman to which she must cling, and which contained beneath Nanny's painstakingly formed words a message which only she could understand.

"I can talk this over with Nanny," she said to herself. "She will tell me what to do. I know she will help me."

She stared out the window, thinking.

Nanny was arriving tomorrow and Iola knew that she would not be at Honeysuckle Cottage early as she had to come from a great distance.

That meant it would be best to visit her on Thursday.

It would give them a day to talk things over.

'It's not long enough,' Iola thought in a sudden panic.

She had to tell Nanny how afraid she was of being married to a man who was old enough to be her father; a man who she was sure wanted her as his wife only for the purpose of giving him an heir. To explain it all would take time.

"How do people have babies? What happens to give one a baby?" Iola puzzled, and knew that this was something else she must ask Nanny.

It was in fact something that had puzzled her for some time, but she had been too embarrassed to ask anyone she knew, certainly not the Governesses who looked down their noses when she even mentioned the word "love."

It was also not the sort of question she could ask Aunt Margaret, who, after all, had never been married herself.

But Nanny would tell her. She would know, and at least if she had to marry that old man with the white beard, she would be prepared for whatever she was in for.

She supposed he would kiss her and they would sleep together in a double bed as her father and mother had done.

She felt herself shudder at the thought.

What would the Lord Lieutenant look like without his clothes?

She had always seen him in the special uniform he wore for important occasions or in the grey topcoat in which he came to the Manor, with a large gold watch-chain across his rather portly stomach.

The idea of him in a nightshirt was a picture from which her thoughts shied away like a nervous horse.

'When he kisses me,' she thought, 'his lips will touch mine.'

She had never seen his lips as they were hidden in his grey moustache, but she supposed somewhere between his moustache and his beard they existed, and again she felt herself shiver.

"He is old! He is old!"

She was sure Nanny would think so, but even if she did, what could either of them do about it?

"I have to talk to Nanny. I have to get to her as soon as possible and spend Thursday and Friday with her," she told herself.

She was sure that such a suggestion would be frowned upon by her father.

She had never been allowed to stay away from home. Even when his other sister had suggested last year that she might stay with her for the Newmarket Races, her father had refused to allow her to go.

"You are far too young to start gadding about," he had said. "You can do all that after you're grown up. Besides, women are a nuisance at race-meetings."

"I should like to go and stay with Aunt Elizabeth, Papa," Iola said wistfully.

"She will ask you again," the General replied. "Write and thank her, and tell her I consider you to be too young. When you are eighteen it will be different."

Although she had obediently written the letter, she had the feeling that when she was eighteen things would not change.

The General disapproved of "gadding about" simply because he himself had no wish to "gad," which was not surprising at his age.

"I will stay with Nanny whatever anyone says," Iola determined.

A sudden thought struck her.

If she left very early the next morning, she would be able to avoid seeing Lord Stoneham and receiving his proposal of marriage.

It was an idea that persisted in her mind but she told herself it was impossible to do anything so revolutionary, as it was against her father's wishes.

Then she knew that she could not and would not agree to marry Lord Stoneham until she had talked it over with Nanny.

"She will understand what I feel, and she will find a way out . . . if there is one."

She remembered the dozens of times that Nanny had saved her from her father's anger or her mother's reproaches when she had done something that was naughty.

This was rather different. Still, in an almost childish manner Iola clung to her belief that Nanny would save her.

There was nobody else who would even begin to understand what she was feeling.

She went down to dinner looking pale and, although her father and aunt were unaware of it, resolute.

She had sat all the afternoon planning what she would do.

If the General had been perceptive, he would have recognised that there was a part of himself in Iola which in an emergency could clearly and directly think out an operation down to the very last detail.

"You are very quiet, Iola," the General boomed at her across the Dining-Room table.

"I expect Iola's feeling a little bewildered," Aunt Margaret said kindly. "You must remember, Alexander, she has at the moment a great deal to think about."

"Yes, of course, of course!" the General agreed, as if the idea had not occurred to him before. "Well, if Stoneham is to be here at twelve I shall have to get up early. I have an appointment to see the builder about that cottage I am repairing."

"I am afraid it is costing you a lot of money," his sister said.

"Far too much," the General agreed. "This chap expects an extortionate amount for labour and he keeps telling me that materials have gone up in price. It certainly does not pay to own cottages these days!"

"I suppose you could always let them fall to the ground," Margaret Herne hazarded.

"And if I do, where will I put my new pig-man?" the General enquired. "I have to house him, whatever it costs."

He drank a little more of his claret before he remembered what had started the conversation.

"Anyway, I can be back here by eleven-thirty," he said, "if I have breakfast at seven-thirty."

He turned his head towards the Butler, who was standing behind his chair.

"Did you hear that, Newton? Breakfast at seven-thirty, and mind it's punctual!"

"I will see to it, Sir."

As everything in the house was always timed exactly on the clock, there was really no need for the General to be so aggressive.

But Iola had often thought that he missed having a great number of troops to order about and therefore had to make do with the small household staff.

She slipped away upstairs immediately after dinner and thought to herself that everything was working out splendidly.

When she reached her bedroom her things were laid out for the night, but none of the housemaids had waited up to help her undress.

It had been her Governess's job to do that, and when the last one had left, six months ago, the housemaids had just assumed that she would look after herself. Iola really preferred it that way.

Now she knew it was definitely a blessing that there was nobody to see what she was about to do.

There was a cupboard at the end of the passage and she dragged from it a large leather trunk which should have been put in the attic a long while ago, where all the luggage was kept.

But this trunk was sometimes used by the General when he stayed at one of his friends' houses for a shoot, and the footman had been too lazy to carry it up more than two flights of stairs.

It was heavy, but Iola pulled it along the passage to her room, then locked her door and started to pack.

She decided that she would take a lot of clothes with her just in case Nanny thought it a good idea for her to go away and not return home until Lord Stoneham no longer wished to marry her.

Iola could not really imagine Nanny giving her such advice nor her father accepting her disappearance, but she was determined to provide for every emergency.

She had worked out that there were three things she could do: first, marry Lord Stoneham as he wished her to do; secondly, stay at Honeysuckle Cottage until the General agreed that there should be no engagement and no marriage, but how she would achieve that she was not quite certain.

Thirdly, go to London and get a job.

This was the vaguest and least considered of the possibilities, because the actual details of what she could do or how she could find employment were completely beyond Iola's comprehension.

Nevertheless, those were the three ideas she would put before Nanny and wait for her judgement in the matter.

She could not believe that Nanny would make her take what superficially seemed the easiest course and marry Lord Stoneham, who became more frightening and more inhuman every time she thought of him.

"As I shall doubtless have no money to buy more

clothes, I must take them all with me," Iola told herself.

There was also on her list the problem of money.

Iola's Godmother had on her death left her a legacy of two hundred pounds.

This was in the Bank and so far she had never needed to draw any of it out.

Aunt Margaret, however, had suggested to the General on Iola's eighteenth birthday that she should have a cheque-book.

"It is what I always longed for myself when I was her age," she said. "But you know, Alexander, how difficult our father was. So I never had one until he was dead."

"What would you want with a cheque-book?" the General growled.

"Well, you may think it is very forward and modern of me, and almost like being a Suffragette," Margaret Herne replied, "but I do think it is slightly degrading for a woman to have to ask a man, whether he is her father or her husband, for everything she needs, even a packet of hair-pins."

"I see nothing degrading about it," the General replied.

"It would be nice," Iola interposed, "to be able to have one's own money to spend on presents. Up to now, although I bought you a Christmas present out of my pocket-money, it was really your money I was spending! Whatever I buy is really paid for by you."

The General considered for a moment, then conceded the point.

"Very well, you shall have your cheque-book," he said, "but you understand you are not to cash a cheque without discussing it with me first."

"No, of course not, Papa."

"I give you fifty pounds a year," the General went on. "That should be enough for any woman."

"Yes, Papa, and it is very generous," Iola said,

"but I have planned a very special birthday present for you and now I can buy it with my own money."

What had happened was that when the moment had come to pay for the cartridge-bag she had bought for him, Iola had not asked permission to cash a cheque, because then he would have been bound to ask what it was for.

She had wanted it to be a surprise, so she had paid for it out of her dress-allowance. But she had always meant to pay herself back when she next went into the main shopping-town, which was Eastbridge.

Now it was with a sense of satisfaction that she realised she had two hundred pounds in the Bank and ten pounds left of her annual allowance.

"I am rich enough to last on my own for quite a long time," she told herself.

But she wondered apprehensively if her father had the power to stop her from drawing out her own money.

Then she told herself that perhaps he would forget about it, at least until she had had a chance to cash a cheque.

She finished packing the trunk and strapped it up. Then she undressed and got into bed.

As she lay in the darkness, she was aware that her heart was beating in an uncomfortable manner and she knew it was because she was frightened.

She was frightened of the future, frightened of running away, and far more frightened of having to marry an old man with a white beard, a man who did not in any way resemble the heroes of her dreams.

Iola clasped her hands together.

"Please, God," she prayed, "make Nanny help me. Make her find a solution. There must be one!"

Chapter Two

Travelling towards Little Waywood in a hired carriage, Iola thought she had been very clever.

She had lain awake planning exactly how she would leave the house and everything had happened just as she had intended.

She waited upstairs until she had seen her father drive away from the front door in his dog-cart, which was a vehicle he particularly fancied driving when he was alone.

Sitting behind was a Tiger—a small groom whose cockaded top-hat seemed too big for him and who was actually older than he looked.

The General appreciated a good horse and the one he now drove had won prizes at the local Shows, which were prominently displayed in his Study.

Iola watched until he turned the corner of the drive, then she ran down the stairs to find Henry the footman.

She knew now that her father had gone Newton would be having his breakfast in the Servants' Hall. Henry was the less intelligent of the two footmen and therefore was less likely to ask questions than James, who was rather sharper.

"Will you order the brake for me, Henry?" she said. "Ask them to bring it to the side-door as quickly as possible. I have to take a trunk on the train. After you have been to the stables, come upstairs and fetch it down from my bedroom."

She repeated herself twice so that Henry would not make a mistake, then hurried back to her room and put on her travelling-cloak which was warm and trimmed with sable.

She wore a small sable hat to match. The fur had belonged to her mother, and as she looked in the mirror Iola thought that she appeared rich and smart and not at all the type of woman who would be looking for employment.

She left a letter for her father propped up on her writing-desk.

She was just picking up her bag and gloves when Henry knocked at the door.

"There is the trunk, Henry," she said. "Carry it down the back-stairs and put it in the brake."

"Yes, Miss," Henry mumbled.

He was a strong boy and he picked up the trunk quite easily although, packed with nearly every gown which Iola possessed, it was very heavy.

She was apprehensive in case he would insist on having James to help him, but he went off down the corridor and she followed him, using the back-stairs herself also, although she thought he might consider her doing so rather strange.

They encountered no-one. Fortunately the upper-servants were all having a late breakfast while the under-maids were cleaning and tidying the Sitting-Rooms.

The brake was already waiting outside the side-door when Iola reached it.

This was, she knew, thanks to her father's dislike of having to wait any longer than was necessary when he sent for a vehicle.

It had therefore become a competition between the grooms to see how quickly they could saddle a horse or put one between the shafts and get it round to the front door.

Henry heaved the trunk into the brake, and as Iola climbed onto the front to sit beside Ben, who was driving, he looked at her in surprise.

"Good-marnin' Miss Iola," he said. "Oi did'n' expec' yer to be a-goin' too. Should Oi fetch a carriage?"

"No, thank you, Ben. I am quite happy to ride on the brake."

"You'll be cold, Miss."

"I will be all right," Iola answered.

There were two rugs provided for those who travelled on the front of the brake, one of wool, the other of a kind of pliable waterproof leather which could be strapped to the sides to keep out the rain and the draughts.

Iola knew that Ben was very surprised that she should travel in such a manner, but it was not his job to argue with his employers and so he set off, and as they turned towards the drive he said:

"'Enry says, Miss, as yer wish t' go t' the station."

"That is right, Ben. I was intending to send this trunk to a friend in London, but I have now decided to accompany it."

Ben was obviously not interested, concerned only with driving the horses, and they rode in silence for six miles to the small town of Eastleigh, where some of the slower trains for London stopped.

Iola was aware that as she had ordered the brake and travelled in it herself, there would be only one coachman driving it.

When she and her aunt drove in the closed Brougham or in the summer in an open Victoria, there was always old Groves the coachman to drive them and one of the other grooms to act as footman.

He was there not only to open the door for them but to unlatch the gates in the Parks through which they must pass if they were calling on any of Aunt Margaret's friends.

When they reached Eastleigh Station it was impossible for Ben to leave the horses, so Iola stepped down and told a porter to lift the trunk from the back of the brake.

He set it on his barrow and pushed it into the station, and only when she knew that Ben had driven away did she say:

"I have changed my mind and will not be travelling by train as I intended to do. I would like a hired carriage."

The porter thought her behaviour was strange but he did not say so. He merely found a cab for her in the stable-yard, heaved her trunk onto the top of it with the help of the driver, and accepted the tip she gave him with a touch of his cap.

The cab-driver, having been told where to go, set off.

They travelled slowly towards Little Waywood, Iola thinking that she had covered her tracks very successfully.

In the note she had written to her father she had said merely that she had to have time to think about the possibility of marrying Lord Stoneham.

She wrote that she had therefore gone away to stay with friends for a few days and asked her father to please explain to His Lordship that she could not take such an irrevocable step without having a little time to get used to the idea.

She knew that every word she wrote would infuriate her father and she could imagine the rage he would be in.

At the same time, there was nothing he could do except rack his brains to think where she might have gone and with whom she might be staying.

He would, Iola was certain, make every effort to make her behaviour seem less reprehensible than it was when he spoke of it to Lord Stoneham.

The cab did not travel quickly; Little Waywood was off the beaten track, and as the lanes approaching it were narrow, the cabby was taking no risks of running into another vehicle.

Therefore it took nearly as long to reach Honeysuckle Cottage as it had taken to travel from the Manor to Eastleigh Station.

At last there was the first glimpse of the Norman Church, the black-and-white Inn on the village green, and then Honeysuckle Cottage, looking more than ever like the gingerbread-house that Nanny had told Iola about when she was small.

They drew up outside and almost for the first time Iola realised that Nanny would not yet be there. She had said she was arriving on Wednesday, which was today, but doubtless she had meant much later in the day.

Even as Iola wondered a little apprehensively how she would be able to get into the house, she saw that the curtains were drawn back on either side of the green painted door, and the next moment she thought she saw a face at the window.

She jumped out of the carriage and ran up the stone path to knock at the door.

Then, as she listened tensely, there were footsteps inside the house, the door opened, and there was Nanny.

"Miss Iola!" she exclaimed. "I wasn't expecting you today."

"I was afraid you would not yet be here, Nanny," Iola replied, hugging her. "But I had to come when I could, which I will explain to you as soon as the man has brought in my trunk."

As she spoke she looked back to see the cabby pull her trunk off the roof and slide it down onto the ground.

"Your trunk, Miss Iola?" Nanny questioned. "Are you staying with me?"

"If you will have me."

"Of course I will, although you may not be very comfortable."

"I want to be with you, Nanny. I will tell you all about it, but let us get the trunk in first."

The cabby struggled up the path making more of a to-do over the trunk than Henry had done.

"Up the stairs, please," Nanny said in her brisk voice. "First room on the right at the top."

The cabby muttered beneath his breath, but did as he was told, negotiating the small narrow stairway with difficulty. A loud thump on the ceiling above Iola's head told her he had managed it.

She paid him what he asked for the fare and tipped him lavishly.

He thanked her in a voice which told her he was surprised at getting such a generous tip from anyone who lived in a cottage, then saluted her respectfully and went back to his cab.

Nanny shut the door behind him.

"Now, what's happened?" she asked. "I know something's up."

"Something is!"

"Then you'd better tell me all about it," Nanny said. "But first sit down. You can take your cloak off in a moment. I've lit the fire. The place was as cold as charity when I got here an hour ago."

"I could not wait until tomorrow," Iola said, "although I knew that was when you would be expecting me. I had to run away as soon as Papa left the house."

"Run away?" Nanny queried.

"Oh, Nanny, only you will understand, and I want to tell you all about it," Iola said.

As she spoke she pulled off her gloves and undid the front of her cloak. Then, as if she wanted to be free of all restrictions, she took her fur hat from her head and put it down on the kitchen-table.

She was seated in front of the stove, which was throwing out a good heat, and Nanny pulled up a hard kitchen-chair to sit opposite her, putting out her hands towards the fire.

As she did so, Iola thought it strange that Nanny should feel so cold when actually the kitchen was quite warm, and she looked at her properly for the first time since she had arrived.

"You are not well, Nanny!" she exclaimed.

As she spoke, she knew that Nanny looked very much older than when she had last seen her.

That had been nearly three years ago and she had seen a change then, but not as much as she saw now.

"It's nothing, Miss Iola," Nanny replied. "I'll be all right."

"What do you mean by 'all right'?" Iola questioned. "Have you been ill?"

"Well, I've been under the weather, so to speak," Nanny answered. "It's my time of life, 'the change' they call it, and all I can tell you is it's not a change for the better!"

"Nanny!" Iola exclaimed in dismay.

Now she could see that Nanny was not only thinner and more lined than she had been before, but she looked definitely unwell, which was something she had never looked before.

"You've not come here to talk about me," Nanny said.

"I am not going to talk about myself until you tell me what is wrong," Iola replied.

"Oh, the Doctor says it's a bit of trouble with my heart," Nanny said in an irritated tone. "I don't listen to 'Old Saw-bones,' as I calls him, as a general rule, but I get some pain from time to time. I think it's indigestion, whatever he may say."

"If it gives you pain, Nanny, it may be serious."

"Well, it's not got to be," Nanny said, "not now when I've got the chance of a lifetime."

"The chance of a lifetime?" Iola repeated. "Oh, Nanny, tell me."

Nanny put down her hands and turned to smile at her.

"First things first," she said. "You tell me your tale and I'll tell you mine."

Iola drew in her breath.

"Nanny, I had to come to you. I know you will not believe it, but Papa insists on my marrying Lord Stoneham."

Nanny looked at her blankly.

"You remember Lord Stoneham, Nanny. The old man with a beard and a wife who had more jewellery than anybody else. I remember you and Rose counting her strings of pearls and Rose said she looked like an Indian Maharanee."

Rose had been the housemaid, and now Nanny exclaimed:

"Of course I remember! But how can you marry him if he's got a wife?"

"Lady Stoneham died a year ago and Lord Stoneham's son was killed in Africa."

"Oh, yes, I remember that now," Nanny said. "It was in all the newspapers. Very brave they said he was, and they gives him a medal after he was dead—not that that did him any good."

"I cannot marry anybody as old as my father, can I, Nanny? Even though Papa thinks he is so important that I ought to be grateful that he wishes to marry me."

"He must be old enough to be your grandfather!" Nanny exclaimed, "Nasty I calls it, an old man running after a girl of your age."

"He is not exactly running after me," Iola said. "He just spoke to Papa, who says I have to marry him."

"So you came to me."

"I came to ask you what I should do."

She saw that Nanny did not understand, and she went on:

"Nobody knows I am here. I left a note for Papa saying I was going to stay with friends until I could think things over. I left the Manor and went to Eastleigh Station."

"To the station?" Nanny queried.

"Then I came here, as you saw, in a hired cab."

"You can't stay here for long," Nanny said. "I'm leaving tomorrow."

"Tomorrow?" Iola cried in consternation.

"I was wondering before you arrived whether I should send you a telegram," Nanny said. "Just in case you would be coming over to see me. My plans have changed, you see."

"But why? What has happened?" Iola asked.

"Well, as I said, it seemed like the chance of a lifetime," Nanny answered. "The little girl I've been looking after has had her sixth birthday and is going to School. Her mother, Lady Lawson, had warned me to start looking out for a new situation, saying she would be happy to help in any way, because she was so grateful for what I'd done for Marigold."

Iola had already heard about Marigold and she said:

"She will miss you, Nanny, as I did."

Nanny accepted this with a nod of her head.

"Well, I'd made a few enquiries and put my name down at the Bureau, when I learns that Sir Wolfe Renton was wanting a Nanny for his child."

Nanny said the name in a manner which told Iola it was important.

"Sir Wolfe Renton!" she repeated. "I seem to have heard of him but I cannot think how."

"He's always in the papers, Miss Iola. He's a friend of the King, one of those financiers he has round him, all rolling in money, and Sir Wolfe is one of the richest."

"I know what you mean," Iola said.

She had heard the General and some of his

friends disparaging the way in which the King, when he was Prince of Wales, had opened the door of Marlborough House to men who had never been admitted to the Social World in the past.

"Things have changed since I was a young man," the General had boomed. "To be accepted at Court in those days, you had to have a decent line of ancestry behind you, besides having served your country with distinction."

He had preened himself a little, as if his words had made him conscious of the long row of medals he was entitled to wear on his chest, and he had continued:

"Now with the King surrounded with men like Rothschild, Cassel, and Oppenheim, who are enveloped in an aura of gold, we Englishmen look like having to take a back-seat."

The General's sentiments had been echoed a thousand times by his friends, and Iola could remember hearing Lady Stoneham say to her aunt:

"Princess Alexandra looked really beautiful, but then she always does! But even her diamonds were eclipsed by those worn by the wives of the Prince's millionaire friends."

Her Aunt Margaret had looked surprised and Lady Stoneham had explained:

"The Rothschilds were there and I have never seen anything so magnificent as her tiara. One diamond—well—it must have been the size of a two-shilling piece!"

Iola had not continued to listen because she had not found it very interesting, but now she remembered the conversation and also a more recent outburst from her father.

He had flung down the *Times* which he had been reading and said furiously:

"Who the devil is this Wolfe Renton who has just been Knighted? What has he done to deserve the K.C.B.?"

This, Iola was aware, was a sore point.

It was the decoration the General had always thought he himself was entitled to when he retired.

For some reason the honour had not been conferred, and when every Honours List appeared he was always fiercely critical of those who received what he had been denied.

"Wolfe Renton!" he had gone on. "What a name to start with! He may be as rich as they say he is, but I cannot believe that any man could make that much money in England today and make it honestly!"

Iola had not answered her father's tirade. She had heard it too often.

It was only now that the name came back to her because it was unusual.

"Tell me about Sir Wolfe Renton, Nanny," she asked.

"I don't know much about him myself," Nanny admitted, "except that when Lady Lawson heard I had the opportunity of going to him, she said:

" 'You must accept this position, Nanny. We will manage for the next month until Marigold goes to School, but you must not miss such an opportunity, which I can assure you is one of a lifetime.'

" 'And why should you think that, M'Lady?' I enquired.

" 'As it happens, I am not only thinking of you—although you know, Nanny, I am determined to find you the sort of position you deserve—but also of Sir Wolfe's poor motherless little daughter.'

" 'I understands, M'Lady,' I said.

" 'His wife died five years ago when their daughter was born,' Her Ladyship went on. 'It was sad for him but worse for the child, and I have often wondered if she was being properly looked after.'

" 'I seem to remember, M'Lady, that you and His Lordship have stayed at Sir Wolfe's house.'

" 'Yes, we have, Nanny, and very magnificent it

is! We have also been to his parties in London, although of course his child stays in the country.'

"Her Ladyship thinks for a moment, then she says:

" 'I remember the child's name now. It is Lucy, a pretty little thing, but rather delicate, I understand.'

" 'That's what I was told, M'Lady,' I says.

" 'It is why her father is sending her to the South of France,' Her Ladyship replied. "I believe he has a very fine Villa there, although I have never seen it.' "

"The South of France!" Iola exclaimed, as if she could no longer keep silent. "Oh Nanny, how exciting for you. It is somewhere I have always longed to go."

"So have I," Nanny agreed. "But I've never until now had a chance to travel."

"Lady Lawson is right. Of course you must go. But why so quickly? Why tomorrow?"

"Well, I understands, from what Sir Wolfe's secretary told me, who I sees in London, that the little girl has a cough that the Doctors don't like. So they're sending her to a warm climate."

"And they want her to leave tomorrow?"

Nanny nodded.

"I'm to catch the Express to Southampton which passes through Eastleigh at nine o'clock. Lucy is being taken to Southampton by the Nanny as is leaving, an old woman, I understand, who says she wasn't going to no foreign parts. She'd rather retire."

"So you got the opportunity to go in her place! How wonderful, Nanny. I am so glad for you!"

Iola smiled mischievously and added:

"As there is no Lady Renton to interfere, you will have everything your own way and you know how you like that."

Nanny smiled in response.

"That's true enough, although as you know, none of my ladies has ever interfered with the Nursery, not even your mother."

"That is because you pleased them so much and they trusted you," Iola said. "And surely Lady Lawson gave you a wonderful reference?"

"It's so good," Nanny admitted, "I'm afraid to show it to anyone, in case they think I've faked it!"

They both laughed, then Iola said in a rather small voice:

"Now, Nanny, tell me what I am to do."

"I don't know, dear, and that's a fact!" Nanny replied.

"If only I could come with you," Iola said with a sigh. "Could you not say you want a Nursery-maid or something?"

"I doubt they'd believe me."

"I do not know why not."

Iola was warm now and she pushed back her cloak and stood up to look in the small mirror which was hung over the mantelshelf in a frame carved and painted with marigolds. She had given it to Nanny one Christmas and had paid for it at the village-store with her own money.

She looked at the reflection of her face and pulled back the sides of her hair.

"If I put my hair up in a bun at the back," she said, "and put your straw-boater on top of my head, I would look just like you when you first came to the Manor."

"Go on with you!" Nanny exclaimed. "I was never as pretty as you, Miss Iola, not even in my hey-day, and now I'm beginning to look so old, my face often frightens me when I see it!"

Iola turned quickly from the mirror to look at Nanny.

"To me it will always be the most beautiful face I have ever seen," she said. "There is love in it and that, as you yourself once told me, is what makes a face beautiful."

"Did I say that?" Nanny questioned. "Well, it's true."

"All the things you have ever said to me have made good sense," Iola said, "and that is why, Nanny, you have to tell me what to do about Lord Stoneham, for it is a question I cannot answer myself."

"Well now, dearie, I shall have to think about it," Nanny said. "Remember, if you don't marry him, your father might choose someone you dislike even more."

"I want to choose my own husband," Iola said sharply. "It is all very well for Papa to be all puffed up with pride because Lord Stoneham wants to marry his daughter, but it is I who have to live with my . . . husband, not Papa."

"No-one's gainsaying that," Nanny replied. "At the same time, dear, you'll be comfortable. You'll be the mistress of a big house. I saw it once. Very impressive it was, and I suppose he'll give you Her Ladyship's jewels to wear."

"The thought of it makes me shudder!" Iola exclaimed. "I should always feel that she resented my wearing them."

"That's silly talk, as you well know," Nanny said. "Work it out, dear; if you refuse to marry His Lordship, the Master could make things very difficult for you."

"Yes, I know," Iola said, "and he has set his heart on the marriage, Nanny. That is what frightens me."

Nanny was silent, wearing what Iola thought of as her "thinking face."

After a moment she said:

"It's hard, very hard on you, and it's not right that spring should mate with winter. It never has been, but if you defy the Master, what can you do? Where can you go?"

"That is why I came to you."

"You can't stay here—not alone."

"I have enough money to last for at least a year," Iola said, "perhaps longer."

"That's not the point," Nanny replied. "Your father will be looking for you and when you don't go back, he'll get the Police to search for you. It'll all be very uncomfortable and cause a scandal."

Iola suddenly knelt down beside Nanny and, putting her arms round her, said:

"I thought of all that during the night. Papa will try to drag me back and force me to marry that horrible old man with the white beard. I feel sick at the very idea. I do not want to marry him, I do not want to have children with him. I want to fall in . . . love."

Her voice broke on the last word and suddenly she was crying against Nanny's shoulder as she had cried when she was a child. Nanny's arms went round her, holding her close.

"There, there," Nanny said soothingly. "Don't take on so. We'll think of something. Don't cry, my dearie. It's not like you to upset yourself like this."

"I . . . I cannot help it," Iola sobbed. "It is happening so quickly . . . and now you are going away."

A fresh burst of tears prevented her from saying any more. Then Nanny said in her most sensible voice:

"Now stop crying, it won't do any good and will merely give you a headache. I'm going to make you a cup of tea and we'll talk this over. There must be a solution somewhere, but I can't think of one at the moment. Now, let me put the kettle on."

Iola sat back on her heels and gave a little laugh that was half a sob.

"It's just like old times, Nanny, to hear you say: "I'll put the kettle on. A cup of tea always seemed to solve everything."

"There's nothing like it for making one think clearly," Nanny said, rising from her chair. "Now get up off the floor, Miss Iola. I haven't had a chance to give this place a good clean since I came back and there's dust everywhere, although I asked Mrs. Briggs next door to look after it for me. But there, you can trust no-one except yourself."

She filled the kettle, set it on the hob, and, taking a clean table-cloth from a drawer in the table, spread it and laid out the tea-things.

"If I'd known you were a-coming," she said, "I'd have bought some of those sugary biscuits you used to like when you were a child. I did get a loaf of new bread as I came from the station, and Her Ladyship gave me some butter and eggs before I left the Castle."

Iola was wiping her eyes.

Her conversation with Nanny did not seem to have got her very far. At the same time, she felt better in herself.

The fear which had been like a lump in her breast ever since yesterday was not so heavy or so painful, and it was almost as if Nanny in her inimitable way had given her hope, although what it might be she could not yet formulate.

The kettle started to boil and Nanny picked up the tea-pot, and as she did so, Iola noticed that she put her hand quickly on her left side.

"What is it, Nanny?" she asked. "Are you in pain?"

"It just catches me," Nanny said impatiently. "It's indigestion, that's what I'm sure it is. Those Doctors know nothing! The medicine he gave me wouldn't cure so much as a headache. It's nothing but pink water, I wouldn't wonder."

She filled the tea-pot and when she came back to the table Iola said:

"You know, Nanny, I think you ought to lie down. You have a long journey in front of you tomorrow and a new charge at the end of it. Go to bed. I will bring you up something to eat."

"The mere idea!" Nanny exclaimed. "And when did you learn to cook, I'd like to know?"

"You will not believe this," Iola answered, "but I have been taking lessons from old Mrs. Huggins."

"She's actually giving them to you?" Nanny enquired. "I thought she never allowed anyone into her kitchen."

Iola gave a little laugh.

"I had to plead with her on my knees. I have always believed that any woman worth her salt should be a good cook, and no-one can say Mrs. Huggins isn't one."

"No, indeed," Nanny agreed. "When your mother was alive they had some real fancy dishes in the Dining-Room, as good as any Chef could produce, people used to say. But then the Master only fancied plain things."

"Very plain," Iola agreed, thinking of the interminable portions of roast beef she had had to consume.

"So you can cook," Nanny said, sitting down rather quickly at the table, which made Iola certain that her pain was still there.

"Aunt Margaret would have tried to stop me," Iola said, "but Papa agreed it was a good thing to learn."

" 'Officers' wives in India have always had to instruct their native servants how to make the most simple dishes,' he said.

"I think he was actually contemplating that I might marry a soldier."

"Perhaps that might still happen," Nanny said consolingly.

"Now that he has Lord Stoneham in mind, he would never listen to any soldier, unless he was a General, and then they would be as old as each other," Iola said despairingly.

"It's unnatural, that's what it is," Nanny said sharply.

Then as her eyes rested on Iola she continued:

"It's because you are so pretty, dearie, much

prettier than I thought you would grow up to be when you were a little girl."

"Do you mean that, Nanny?"

"I mean it," Nanny replied, "and I only wish your mother could see you now. She often said to me: 'Iola's going to be pretty, Nanny, but pretty women always have problems.'

" 'Which are invariably men,' I replied, and your mother laughed."

"You were only predicting what has come true," Iola said mournfully. "Men are my problem at the moment, or rather one man, an old man with a white beard! I cannot marry him!"

"Now drink your tea," Nanny said. "Cut yourself a slice of bread. I've a pot of strawberry jam put away somewhere that I made last time I was here. It won't have hurt for the keeping."

"If I eat too much for 'elevenses' I shall not have room for luncheon, and I am sure you are making something delicious, Nanny . . . unless you would like me to cook for you?"

"It'll be over my dead body when you wait on me in my own kitchen," Nanny replied. "And as it happens, I've already decided what we shall eat."

"What is that?" Iola asked.

"It'll be a surprise," Nanny replied.

It was as if they were back in the Nursery, and it was Nanny's surprises that made Iola hungry when otherwise she was finicky about her food.

The day passed quickly.

They talked and talked and somehow it always got back to the same question, to which there appeared to be no answer—how could Iola avoid marrying Lord Stoneham?

It was after tea that they went upstairs for Nanny to undo the straps on Iola's trunk and take out the things she would need for the night.

"Surely this is your best room?" Iola said. "It is really yours."

"There's not much difference in them," Nanny replied, "and actually I've got my things packed and ready next door."

"Let me look at them," Iola said.

Nanny's trunk was open and it was filled, Iola could see, with her blouses and skirts. There were white ones and grey ones, and there was a pile of stiffly starched white aprons which Nanny wore in the Nursery besides a flannel one which she put on when it was bath-time.

Right on the top was one of Nanny's stiff belts which she always wore round her waist and which had a pretty silver filigree buckle that Iola had known ever since she was tiny.

"You still have your pretty buckle, Nanny!" she exclaimed.

"I wouldn't part with that for all the tea in China!" Nanny answered. "It belonged to my mother and her mother before her, and a nice bit of silver it is too."

Iola put the stiff belt round her own waist.

"Nanny, you have lost weight!" she said. "My waist used to be smaller than yours. Now this belt fits me exactly!"

"So it does!" Nanny exclaimed. "But I expect I'll soon put on what I've lost, when I get to the sunshine. This indigestion is doubtless due to the cold."

She gave a little smothered groan as she spoke and sat down on the bed.

"I am sure you ought to see another Doctor, Nanny," Iola said.

"I've seen one," Nanny answered, "and I tell you he talked a lot of nonsense. The truth is I need a holiday and to get away from the stairs in the Castle. On the fourth floor we were up and down and I had to trot a dozen times a day!"

"The fourth floor!"

"It was beginning to make me feel my age."

"I am sure the Villa in the South of France will

not be nearly as high as that," Iola said. "And for goodness' sake, if Sir Wolfe is so rich, make him give you a Nursery-maid to do your running up and down for you."

"I will!" Nanny said.

Iola sighed.

"I wish it could be me."

"That would be a nice scandal, wouldn't it?" Nanny remarked. "Sir Wolfe Renton, friend of His Majesty, taking a young Society Lady into his Villa and pretending he is not aware of it. Do you suppose anyone would believe that story?"

"No, but how much they would enjoy talking about it!" Iola said with a smile.

She gave a little cry.

"Dear Nanny, I still miss the way you used to gossip and make everything sound so amusing. Aunt Margaret only repeats everything she hears in a shocked voice, although she enjoys being scandalised."

"You know as well as I do that I oughtn't to repeat any gossip I hear," Nanny remarked. "But my tongue runs away with me."

"It always did!" Iola laughed.

She turned toward the door.

"I am going to change to another gown," she said. "Not because I am impressing you with how smart I am, but because I think I ought to be careful of this one, which may have to last me a long time."

"What are you thinking of doing?" Nanny asked sharply.

"I am thinking that after you have gone, perhaps I could stay here another night, then go to London."

"Now you'll do nothing of the sort!" Nanny said firmly. "I've never heard of such a thing! How do you think you can look after yourself in a big place like that? Besides, who would employ you without a reference?"

"I am sure I could find something to do."

"And I'm sure you'd get into trouble," Nanny retorted.

She paused for a moment, then she said:

"I'm afraid there's nothing you can do but go home. Talk to the Master quietly and sensibly, and say that while you'll marry His Lordship, you think it only right that you should have a long engagement, of at least a year."

"Do you think Papa would agree to that?"

"I see no reason why he shouldn't," Nanny replied, "but you'll have to handle him in the right way. Coax him, dearie; it were never any use in upsetting the Master. It merely makes him more determined not to be beaten down."

"That is exactly what he will do to me," Iola said in a frightened voice. "He will beat me down . . . he will make me agree to what he wants, and almost before I know what is happening . . . I shall find myself married!"

"Well, things might be worse," Nanny said, "and perhaps His Lordship's so old he'll not be too demanding."

"In what way?" Iola asked.

She knew as she asked the question that Nanny was not going to give her a straight answer. While she felt for words, Iola said:

"There is something I wanted to ask you, Nanny. What happens when one is married and wants to have a baby?"

She could see that Nanny was surprised at her question. Then she said:

"I think that's something we'll talk about later. Go and change your gown as you suggested, and I'll start cooking the dinner. We've both got to get to bed early tonight."

"I do not mind what time we go to bed," Iola replied. "I want to stay with you, Nanny, every moment I can."

As she spoke, she thought she was being selfish.

Nanny looked tired and unwell and Iola was quite certain, although she would not say so, that her side was troubling her.

Iola went into the small room next door and heard Nanny go very slowly down the stairs.

It might have been because they were so narrow and twisting, but she was almost certain that there was another reason.

'I must not upset her,' she thought. 'It is not fair to inflict all my problems on her.'

For the first time in her life she was thinking of Nanny as a person rather than someone who was there to give her love, comfort, and a sense of security.

"If Nanny says I must go back, I suppose I must," she told herself.

She felt herself shiver at the thought of what was waiting for her, not only her father's anger because she had run away, but also Lord Stoneham.

If she said she would marry him she supposed he would kiss her, and she felt herself shudder with repugnance at the very idea of it.

'I cannot let him! I cannot let him touch me!' she thought in a sudden panic.

She had already taken off her gown and she thought that because she was frightened she would run downstairs to the kitchen just as she was and tell Nanny what she was feeling.

Then something stopped her.

This was her problem and she had to decide it for herself.

"I will talk to Nanny again after supper," she decided. "Perhaps at the last moment she will find a way!"

The sands of time were running out. Iola had thought she would have several days with Nanny but now there were only hours left, hours in which they must both sleep, and Nanny at any rate was to leave at eight o'clock tomorrow morning so as not to miss the Express to Southampton.

"Why, why can she not take me with her?" Iola cried silently in her heart.

Then she knew that the one thing she must not do was to jeopardise Nanny's reputation for honesty and straight-forwardness.

That she had come here might make her father angry with Nanny and that would be unforgivable.

"This is my problem, my problem," Iola said over and over again.

Even as she said it, it came to her mind that once again, saying little, but really just because she was there, Nanny had put everything into its proper perspective and made her see things in a very different way from what she had intended.

"The truth is," she told herself, "that in the future I have to stand on my own feet. There is no-one to whom I can cling, no-one who can decide things for me."

She gave a deep sigh and went on:

"There is just me . . . and in consequence I feel very small and insignificant . . . and, worse than . . . anything else . . . helpless!"

Chapter Three

Iola woke with a start, thinking she had heard a noise, then she remembered where she was and thought it must be very early in the morning.

She sat up and lit the candle beside her bed and saw from her watch that it was just after half-past-five.

This meant, she thought, that Nanny would be getting up, and she decided that she would get up too, as she wished to spend every second that she could with her before she left.

Last night they had sat talking for a long time and finally, because she had pressed her and pressed her, Nanny had conceded that she would ask Sir Wolfe Renton if he would consider employing a Nursery-Governess for his daughter.

"You'll have me out of a job, that's what you'll do!" Nanny said, but she was smiling and Iola knew that she was protesting automatically.

"You know I would not do that, Nanny, and you can explain, if you like, that I am young and need training, and that I want to be with you. As he is so rich and money is no object, he should realise that a child of five needs proper lessons."

"Perhaps she has a Governess already," Nanny said, "although they never mentioned it at the interview."

"If there is, you must just shove her out and push me in," Iola said irrepressibly.

Nanny laughed.

"Shall I say I'll see what I can do, but I make no promises. Employers are funny people, they don't like being managed, especially gentlemen."

Nanny paused, then she said almost severely:

"If Sir Wolfe refuses, then you promise me that you'll go home!"

"I will wait until I hear from you," Iola replied. "I expect the yacht will stop at various places on the way to the South of France and you can get one of the sailors to send a telegram for you. I will give you the money."

"I've plenty of my own," Nanny said proudly. "Lady Lawson was very generous when I left. She gave me far more than I ever expected to get as a present from anybody."

"She appreciated you, Nanny, as I do," Iola said, "and I shall pray, I shall pray hard as you taught me to do, that Sir Wolfe will say: 'What a wonderful idea! Of course Lucy must have a Nursery-Governess!' "

Nanny laughed again.

"You're making up stories as you used to do when you were a little girl."

"As you taught me to do," Iola retorted.

They sat talking until Nanny said:

"Now come along, Beddy-byes!" just as she used to say when Iola was a baby.

When they got upstairs Iola put her arms round Nanny and hugged her.

"I love you, Nanny, and at the moment I can imagine nothing more wonderful than to be with you, even if I have to scrub floors to do so."

"That's something you'll never do! Not while I'm there!" Nanny retorted. Then she said:

"Whatever happens, whatever you have to do, you must try to make the best of it. I know it'll not be easy, but nothing is, in life. Courage will always get you to the top of the mountain. Never forget that."

"I will remember," Iola said slowly, almost as if Nanny were making her take a vow.

Now she washed in cold water because she was sure Nanny would be annoyed if she skipped washing, even though it was very chilly in the bedroom and the frost had made patterns all over the window.

When she was dressed, she opened the door and went to the top of the stairs and listened. She expected to hear Nanny down below.

There was silence and there was no light coming from the kitchen.

'I must have been mistaken,' Iola thought, 'and she is not yet awake.'

She had carried the candle in her hand as she left the bedroom and now she knocked on the door on the other side of the stairs.

There was no answer and she opened it.

The candlelight showed her that Nanny was still in bed.

"Nanny!" she exclaimed. "I am sure it is time for you to get up!"

There was no reply and she thought it strange as Nanny was a very light sleeper and awoke at the first movement from one of her charges.

Iola crossed to the bed.

As she did so, she saw that Nanny was lying on her back. Her eyes were closed and there was a smile on her lips.

"Nanny!" she said again.

Then something made her draw in her breath and she stood very still.

Slowly, because her hand was trembling, she put the candle down on the bedside-table, then put out her hand to touch Nanny's cheek.

It was cold....

* * *

Iola felt as if she had taken part in a strange dream ever since she had gone into Nanny's room and found that she was dead.

For a moment she had thought she could not believe her eyes and that she must be imagining something so ridiculous.

How could Nanny, who had always been so alive, so full of fun, be dead?

And yet she knew unmistakably that she had died in her sleep and, because of the smile on her lips, that it had been a happy death.

She was dead, and as Iola went down on her knees she knew she had lost a person who was completely irreplaceable in her life and whom she loved more than she had ever loved anybody, even her mother.

Then as she thought she must burst out crying, Nanny's words the night before came back to her:

"Courage will always get you to the top of the mountain."

It was courage she must have now, courage to behave properly, as Nanny would have wished, not hysterically or thinking only of herself.

"Oh, Nanny, how could you leave me?" she found herself saying in a whisper.

Then she knew that was selfish and that Nanny would have left her anyway.

She had never really believed that she would be able to join her in the South of France. It had just been a child's dream, a fairy-tale she had made up to make things seem better.

All that was left for her now was to go home and persuade her father, as Nanny had suggested, that she should have a long engagement.

'There is nothing else I can do,' she thought despairingly.

She clasped her hands together and prayed for

Nanny, and as she did so she felt that she was almost praying to her rather than to God.

Then as she rose to her feet, she thought she must arrange Nanny's Funeral.

She supposed she would have to find the Vicar of Little Waywood and tell him what had happened.

She picked up the candle from beside the bed and, giving a last glance at Nanny, she thought how she looked younger than she had last night and the lines seemed to have gone from her face.

She looked happy, there was no doubt about that.

As Iola did not dare to look at her for long, for fear that she would cry, she turned away to leave the room, and as she did so, she saw Nanny's trunk open and the clothes in which she was to travel to Southampton lying ready on a chair.

Beside it was the little black bonnet with ribbons that tied under her chin which Nanny wore in the winter.

Her gloves and handbag stood on the table, and Iola knew that inside was a ticket which, she had told her last night, she had already been given for the train journey.

"I'm going Second Class," she had told Iola, "and there'll be somebody to meet me at Southampton to take me to the dock. I'm looking forward to being on the yacht. I have never seen one, but I feels it must be something like a travelling house."

"Suppose you are sea-sick?" Iola had teased.

"I doubt if I'll be that," Nanny had replied. "When I was a child I used to beg, borrow, or steal every half-penny I could, so that I could swing on the Big Wheel that came to Eastleigh every year with the Circus. Hours I used to spend on it, if I had the chance! Some of the other children were sick, but not me."

It was sad that Nanny would never see her "travelling house." It would have been so exciting for her, and Iola added to herself:

"Just as it would have been exciting for me, if I could have gone with her."

It suddenly struck her that she would have to let Sir Wolfe Renton know that Nanny would not be coming.

The child would be waiting on the yacht at Southampton, and if Nanny did not turn up, who would look after little Lucy?

'I will send a telegram,' Iola decided.

She supposed she would have to go into Eastleigh to do that and thought it might be dangerous. Somebody might recognise her, in which case they might tell her father and he would know she was not in London but staying locally.

'I cannot go back yet, not so quickly,' Iola thought, 'not now that Nanny is dead. I must have time to think, time to prepare myself for what I have to say to Papa about a long engagement.'

Then as she looked at Nanny's handbag again, the idea came to her like a flash of lightning.

Why should she send a telegram? Why not go herself and suggest that she should look after Lucy, at least until they could find somebody else?

It was almost like seeing the plot in a book unfold itself in front of her eyes.

She would not say that Nanny was dead, because in that case they would want to replace her immediately with somebody older and experienced.

No, she would say that Nanny was ill and therefore, until she was well enough to travel, she had come in Nanny's place to look after Lucy.

It would be impossible anyway for them to get a replacement while they were at sea, and if they thought Nanny was to join them a little later, in the South of France, why should they trouble to engage somebody else?

"I will go. I will go in Nanny's place, and if they think I am too young, which they will, they will know it is only a temporary arrangement, and so Sir Wolfe is not likely to worry unduly."

Because the idea seemed to present itself like a lifeline to a drowning man, Iola grasped at it.

For some minutes she still hesitated, thinking, staring at Nanny's clothes lying on the chair.

Then again she remembered Nanny saying:

"Courage will always get you to the top of the mountain."

"I will do it!" Iola said aloud.

She turned towards the bed as she spoke, and as she saw her in the faint light of the candle, she felt that Nanny was smiling at her encouragingly.

She picked up her clothes and carried them into the next room.

It took her only a few minutes to take off the gown she was wearing and put on Nanny's stiff grey alpaca, which was her best and which she wore on Sundays.

It was lined and it fastened high at the neck. As Iola glanced at herself in the mirror, she realised that she must do what she had talked of doing yesterday, and pull her hair back from her face.

She brushed it back from the sides and forehead, twisting it as tightly as she could into a bun, and then because her hair was long and thick she had to find a large number of extra hair-pins.

She thought that although it was a severe style, it did not make her look any older.

"It will look better when I wear a bonnet," she told herself.

She quickly packed her own gown in her trunk and put on top of it the cape and the little sable hat that went with it.

'I will take my clothes with me,' she thought, 'in case I am turned away immediately and sent home on the next train.'

Even if Sir Wolfe did anything quite so drastic,

she would still have had the excitement of going South in a yacht, and that would take, she calculated, at least a week.

'It will give me time to think,' she thought reassuringly.

After a last glance at herself in the mirror and thinking how strange she looked with her eyes large and worried in her pointed face, she picked up the candle and started down the stairs.

As she did so she heard sounds below in the kitchen.

'Somebody is there,' she thought in sudden fear.

She wondered who it could be and for one startled moment she thought perhaps she had made a mistake and Nanny was not dead but had gone downstairs to prepare breakfast.

Then she remembered that Nanny had spoken of a Mrs. Briggs who looked after the cottage when she was not there.

'That is who it must be,' Iola thought sensibly.

At the same time, her heart was still beating uncomfortably because she had been afraid.

She walked down the stairs.

In the kitchen by the light of the lamp she saw an elderly grey-haired woman at the stove.

"Good-morning!" Iola said. "You must be . . . Mrs. Briggs."

She was aware that her voice quivered a little and she felt the blood rise in her cheeks as the woman turned round.

"Goodness!" she exclaimed. "Ye startled me! I were expecting Miss Dawes!"

"I am a friend of Miss Dawes."

"I were told her had a visitor," Mrs. Briggs said. "Pleased to meet ye. I can see ye're a Nanny as well."

"Y-yes . . . that is true," Iola said, "but I am . . . afraid I have very . . . bad news."

Mrs. Briggs straightened herself.

"Bad news?"

"Nanny . . . died last . . . night."

In spite of every resolution Iola's voice broke on the words.

"Died? Are ye saying Miss Dawes has died?" Mrs. Briggs questioned, as if she could not believe her ears.

Iola could not answer. It was somehow worse having to say the words than seeing Nanny dead in the silence of the little bedroom.

She sat down at the table and put her hands up to her eyes.

Mrs. Briggs picked up the lamp which was standing on the dresser and, without saying any more, went up the stairs.

While she was away Iola cried helplessly, knowing that she should control herself but finding it impossible.

Mrs. Briggs came down again.

"Her looks ever so happy," she said as she came into the kitchen. "It's a shock, I understands that. I'll make ye a cup of tea."

It was so exactly what Nanny would have said in the circumstances that it made Iola want to cry more than ever.

With what was almost a superhuman effort she managed to say:

"I was going to . . . f-find the Vicar to arrange about her . . . Funeral."

"I'll do that," Mrs. Briggs said. "I knows him well, a fine gentleman, an' he does the Service beautiful! No-one like him in these parts."

It was then that Iola knew she could leave everything in Mrs. Briggs's capable hands.

She told her that she had been going to travel with Nanny to Southampton and that she had to catch the train at nine o'clock.

"I knows that," Mrs. Briggs said. "Mr. Herbert tells as I were a-coming here that he be a-bringing his cart round at eight o'clock to pick up Miss Dawes. He's the Carrier. Always willing t' oblige."

Iola travelled with Mr. Herbert on the front of his cart and the back was piled up with parcels he had to deliver to different places in Eastleigh and two boxes which were to be sent by train.

"Ye look after her, Mr. Herbert," Mrs. Briggs said when they left "and see her has a comfortable seat in a 'Ladies Only' carriage."

She smiled, however, as she added to Iola:

"Ye be a bit young to be travelling on yer own, an' far too pretty, if I may say so."

Mr. Herbert, who was a portly man with, Iola learnt, eight children, thought the same thing.

"Be careful o' them Frenchies!" he warned when she told him where she was going. "You can't trust them foreigners from all I hears. Keep 'em at arm's length, and the longer yer arm, th' better!"

He laughed at his own joke until he coughed, and Iola felt like coughing too, because it was so cold.

Nanny's serge cape was not nearly as warm as her own and by the time they reached Eastleigh she thought that the tip of her nose was so cold it might fall off.

It was difficult, however, to think of anything except that she was leaving Nanny behind and setting off on what she knew was really a mad-cap, crazy adventure.

Yet, whatever happened, it was better than having to brave her father's wrath at her going away without his permission or to listen to Lord Stoneham's proposal of marriage.

There was only one other woman in the carriage besides herself, a tight-lipped elderly one who, Iola found to her relief, had no wish to talk to a stranger.

She seated herself in a corner where she could

stare out at the snow-covered country through which they were passing, aware how cold she was but realising now it was more because of shock than the actual temperature.

Mrs. Briggs had forced her to eat a little breakfast, although she felt as if every mouthful would choke her, and she wanted only to drink the strong warm tea, heavily laced with sugar, which the older woman believed, as Nanny had done, was a panacea for every ill.

"How can I have done anything so reprehensible as to run away, to leave everything behind me that is familiar?" Iola asked herself.

Then she remembered that what she was really leaving behind her was Lord Stoneham, and that was something she need not regret even for a moment.

She felt as if she had indeed become a different person, the person she was pretending to be, a young nurse-maid who was travelling to Southampton almost on an errand of mercy, because Nanny could not bear to let her new employers down.

"I must be word-perfect with my story!"

She decided she would be a relative of Nanny and call herself "Dawes."

"That was why I was with her when she was taken ill."

It sounded plausible.

"I am looking for a situation, and because there was no time for Sir Wolfe, even if he had been told Nanny could not come, to find anyone else, she sent me."

'He ought to be grateful,' she thought, and added reassuringly that he would be.

It was a long way to Southampton, made longer because the train went so slowly.

At noon they stopped at a large station and Iola learnt that there would be time for her to get something to eat.

By this time she was quite hungry and she bought a sandwich and a bun besides hurriedly drinking a cup of hot coffee.

She felt better when she got back into the carriage, although the other occupant gave her a disapproving look as she ate the food she had brought with her.

One thing was fortunate, Iola thought—she had plenty of money.

She had left ten pounds for Mrs. Briggs to pay for the Funeral.

"It won't cost all that!" Mrs. Briggs had protested, in astonishment.

"I want Nanny to have the best Funeral possible," Iola replied, "and if there is any money to spare, please spend it on flowers. She . . . loved flowers."

Mrs. Briggs looked at the ten golden sovereigns as if they were diamonds.

"I don't know what Miss Dawes would say at such extravagance," she said. "Generous she were, if 'twas necessary, but careful, so to speak."

"There is something else," Iola said hastily, having just thought of it. "I must pay you, Mrs. Briggs."

"Ye didn't need to do that . . ." Mrs. Briggs began, but Iola swept her protests to one side.

She had already looked in Nanny's handbag and saw that there was twenty pounds in it, and she knew that this was the large gift which Nanny had received from Lady Lawson.

She insisted on giving Mrs. Briggs two guineas for herself.

"Will you please look after the cottage," she said. "I do not know whether Nanny has any relations who will claim it, but until we find if there is one, I will be responsible for it."

As she spoke, she thought that it was somewhere she could always come if she was desperate as she had been yesterday.

" 'Twas a pleasure to do anything for Miss Dawes," Mrs. Briggs said, "but I ain't going to pretend that the extra money hasn't made a difference to the pension I gets from the gentleman where I worked for thirty years. Money don't go far these days."

"I will send you a guinea every month," Iola promised.

"Ye sound as if ye've got a good job to go to," Mrs. Briggs said curiously.

"I hope that is what it proves to be," Iola replied.

As the train went on again, she was not worrying so much whether her job would be a good one, but whether she would be able to stay away from England long enough for Lord Stoneham to give up wishing to marry her.

She was certain that her father would keep him from knowing the truth for a long time, but he would not be able to do so forever.

Then surely any man, especially one as important as Lord Stoneham, would feel insulted that the girl he had chosen to be his wife preferred to disappear rather than accept him as her husband.

"It is only a question of time before he finds somebody else," she reassured herself.

But she knew she was still afraid.

* * *

The train was two hours late arriving at Southampton, and by that time daylight was fading and the gas-lamps in the station made it seem bizarre and gave it an air of unreality.

Iola felt, even more insistently than she had before, that she was taking part in a dream that had no substance in truth.

She picked up her gloves, collected her handbag, and waited until the train came to a standstill.

Then she stood up, feeling reluctant to step out onto the platform and knowing that now the difficulties of her enterprise would really begin.

There seemed to be a seething mob of people, but actually there had been few travellers in the train and the majority of those waiting on the station were porters.

"Porter, Lady? Porter?"

There were several of them addressing her all at once. Then she heard a voice calling out above the noise of the rest:

"Miss Dawes! Miss Dawes! Anyone 'ere called Miss Dawes?"

It took Iola a moment to remember that that was who she was.

She put up her hand and made a little murmur, and one of the porters beside her shouted:

"'Ere she be, Bill!"

A porter pulling his truck behind him came towards her.

"Ye be Miss Dawes?" he asked.

"Yes," Iola replied.

"There be a gent'man waitin' for ye."

As he spoke he pointed to where, standing back a little from the train, was a man wearing a bowler-hat, who at a glance Iola realised was a senior servant, perhaps a Butler, but she was not certain if one had a Butler aboard a yacht.

"Oi'll get yer trunks, Miss," the porter said. "Be they labelled?"

"Yes," Iola answered. "'Miss Dawes, passenger to Southampton.'"

"Oi'll find 'em," the porter said, and moved away with his barrow.

Feeling a little awkward, Iola walked down the platform to where the man in the bowler-hat was waiting.

He was watching the other passengers and she was close to him before he saw her and turned his head to stare at her in astonishment.

He was a middle-aged man with a wrinkled face.

"I think you are waiting for me," Iola said.

"You're not Miss Dawes!" he exclaimed incredulously.

"I . . . am," Iola replied, "but not the one you were expecting."

She saw that he did not understand, and she explained:

"The Miss Dawes who was engaged is ill. I have come in her place."

"Well, now I understand," the man said. "You took me by surprise, seeing as I was expecting someone a good deal older. So Miss Dawes is ill! Sorry to hear that. The Master won't be pleased. He doesn't like his plans being upset."

"That is why Miss Dawes thought that instead of causing any inconvenience at the last moment, I should come in her place until she was well enough to join you."

"That was kind of her, I'm sure," the man said. "Well, let's introduce ourselves. I'm Mr. Carter, Sir Wolfe's personal valet. And what's your name?"

"My name is Dawes too. I am a relative of Nanny's."

"Well, that makes it easy, at any rate," Mr. Carter said. "Ah, here's your luggage. We'll have to put our best foot forward, so to speak. You're late!"

"The train went very slowly, owing, I understand, to snow on the line."

"Snow, fog, or tempest," Mr. Carter said, "you're still late, and Sir Wolfe's insistent on punctuality."

They walked quickly to the entrance to the station, followed by the porter.

There was a smart carriage waiting for them drawn by two horses and there was a footman on the box.

The latter jumped down and opened the carriage door for Iola, and when she was inside she heard Mr. Carter say to him:

"There's two trunks. We were only expecting one

but you can't leave it behind. We'll have to have it inside."

"I'll have it by me feet up front," the footman replied. "It's not far."

"That's all right then," Mr. Carter said.

Iola saw him tip the porter, then he got into the carriage beside her.

"Travelling in style, aren't we?" he said. "Sir Wolfe had this carriage to meet him yesterday. I thought I might as well use it to meet you."

He spoke as though he was bestowing a favour upon her, and Iola said:

"Thank you."

"Now there's no need to feel nervous," Mr. Carter said, "but I warn you Sir Wolfe won't like your being so late or the fact that you are not the person he was expecting."

"Thank you for telling me."

"Have you ever been in a yacht before?"

"No."

"Well, you'll have a surprise when you see ours. It's the finest yacht of its kind in the whole of the British Isles. We've got some innovations that no-one else has thought of as yet. It's just like the Master. He likes to move with the times, or rather be ahead of them. He keeps us on our toes."

Mr. Carter stopped speaking for a moment, then he said:

"As you are young, I'll give you a tip. Don't argue with him. Just agree to anything he suggests. He pays well and doesn't begrudge his staff any reasonable comfort, but he likes to get his own way."

"Thank you for telling me," Iola said again.

"He won't like the change of plans, that's for sure," Mr. Carter went on, as if he was following his own train of thought, "but it can't be helped, although it's inconvenient, very inconvenient."

If he knew the truth, Iola thought, he might think it was more inconvenient still.

She had not wanted to cry during the journey because of the hard-faced woman on the other side of the carriage, but now for a moment she felt the tears blinding her eyes.

'I am tired, and it is the shock,' she thought sensibly. 'I must be very calm and self-controlled until I have actually been accepted as the child's Nurse.'

Aloud she asked:

"Will the Nanny who brought the little girl down to Southampton be there when we arrive?"

She had a sudden fear in case Sir Wolfe would refuse to allow her to stay and at the last moment persuade Lucy's old Nanny to go with them to the South of France.

Mr. Carter coughed.

"As a matter of fact," he said, "one of the reasons why your being late is so inconvenient is that Nanny had to leave an hour-and-a-half ago in the only good train back to London. But we expected you at any moment."

"So Lucy is alone with her father?"

"There's plenty of people on board to look after her," Mr. Carter replied. "Pretty child, she is. Taking in her ways, and we're all real fond of her."

There was a warmth in his voice that Iola liked.

"I am sure I shall become fond of her too," she said.

She had already told herself that she would look after Lucy as Nanny had looked after her.

She would love her and make up to her for having no mother and for losing Nanny, although she would not be aware of it.

'At least I have a fund of stories to tell her,' she had thought in the train.

It was dark by the time they had travelled a little way from the station.

By the gas-lamps it was difficult to see what the town looked like but Iola was conscious of the great piles of mushy dirty snow piled on each side of the road.

She was cold and she thought that she would be colder still when they put to sea.

Now they were arriving at the dock and she had a glimpse of huge ships towering high in the air, their lights glimmering on the water beneath them.

The horses came to a standstill and Mr. Carter got out.

"Here we are!" he said. "And you are in for a pleasant surprise."

Iola hoped it would be pleasant as she stepped out and felt a sharp wind blowing in her face.

There was a gang-plank in front of her and she walked up it, conscious as she did so that the yacht was very much bigger than she had expected. In fact, if it had not been for the comparison with the other great ships she had just passed, she would have thought it was enormous.

There were several sailors standing about on deck, but Carter was at her side and he said firmly:

"This way, Miss Dawes."

There was a door which he opened for her and Iola found herself in what appeared to be a hall with steps going down into the bowels of the ship.

"I expect you'd like to go to your cabin first," Mr. Carter said.

"Oh, yes, please," Iola answered.

He indicated the steps, and as he did so, a man came hurrying towards them.

He was in uniform and Iola thought he was a Junior Officer of some sort.

"There you are, Mr. Carter!" he exclaimed. "And about time, too, if I may say so. The Captain has been ordered to put to sea immediately you come aboard."

"We're here," Mr. Carter replied.

"What kept you?"

"The train was late."

"I might have guessed that was the excuse! The owner's behaving as if you had absconded with the Crown Jewels!"

Mr. Carter laughed.

"Well, we're here now, so full-steam ahead, as you say!"

He was however talking to thin air, as the Officer had vanished, and Iola proceeded down below.

She walked along a narrow passageway and Mr. Carter opened a door halfway down it.

"This is your cabin, Miss Dawes, although I suppose I should call you 'Nanny,' and Miss Lucy's next door. The cabins communicate."

He led the way into a small but to Iola luxurious cabin. It had a bed when she had expected a bunk, but she could see that the furniture was fitted to the walls and the curtains were of a pretty chintz.

She barely had time to look round her before Mr. Carter opened a door at the side and revealed a very much larger cabin.

This was obviously intended for the child, as there were a number of expensive toys lying about and a much smaller bed set against one of the walls.

Seated on the floor, a doll in her arms, was an exceedingly attractive little girl.

She had dark hair, which Iola had not expected, and seated beside her also on the floor was a young servant dressed in a white coat with polished buttons.

He scrambled to his feet when she appeared and Mr. Carter said:

"So you've been looking after her, have you, Harold?"

"Yes, Mr. Carter, and very good she's been, haven't you, Miss Lucy?"

"I'm always good," Lucy replied.

"Of course you are," Mr. Carter said, "and here's your new Nanny. Come and say how-do-you-do to her."

Lucy looked at Iola but made no effort to rise.

"You're not a Nanny," she said. "You're too young. Nannies are old."

Mr. Carter and Harold both laughed.

"Isn't she a one?" Mr. Carter said to Iola. "Sharp as a needle! Never misses a thing!"

He crouched down in front of Lucy and said:

"Come on! This is a Nanny, even if she's a young one."

"I don't believe you!" Lucy said. "You're playing a trick on me."

Iola was wondering what she could say and how she would convince this precocious child that she was in fact a Nanny, when the other door of the cabin opened and a voice asked:

"Why was I not told you had arrived?"

Mr. Carter turned round quickly and Harold seemed to fade into the background.

Standing in the open doorway of the cabin was a man who looked very different from what Iola had expected.

It had been hard to visualise what Sir Wolfe Renton would look like, but, because his name was always associated with the Rothschilds and the other great financiers she had seen caricatured in the newspapers or sketched in the *Illustrated London News,* she had supposed he would look like them.

They were always depicted as short, paunchy, and with a large nose.

Sir Wolfe, on the contrary, was tall, broad-shouldered, and decidedly good-looking.

He was also far younger than she had anticipated, although she had learnt that he was the youngest of the millionaires who surrounded the King.

He might not be an elderly man but he was, Iola thought, one of the most awe-inspiring she had ever seen.

He was frowning and his dark eye-brows seemed almost to meet across the bridge of his nose. His eyes, dark too and strangely penetrating, seemed to look at her as if they stripped away every pretence and saw the truth far below the surface.

He was wearing a yachting-jacket with brass buttons and as he walked farther into the cabin he seemed to dwarf everything and everybody with his personality.

He looked at Iola and there was no doubt that he was surprised by her appearance.

"You are not the Nurse my secretary engaged!" he said sharply.

"There has been a little . . . trouble, Sir . . ." Mr. Carter began.

"The woman can speak for herself, presumably!" Sir Wolfe interrupted.

"Yes, Sir," Mr. Carter replied quickly.

"You may go!"

It was an order.

Mr. Carter, followed by Harold, seemed to vanish from the cabin, and as the door closed behind them, Sir Wolfe said:

"Now I would like an explanation."

"Nanny Dawes was . . . taken ill . . . she did not wish to let you down . . . and so she sent . . . me to look after . . . your daughter until she is . . . well enough to join you. . . ."

"And that necessitated your being two hours late!"

"I could not travel quicker than the train was able to do," Iola replied.

Even as she spoke, she thought her answer sounded impertinent, and after a moment added: "Sir."

She thought he looked at her critically.

"I imagine you have no experience in looking after a child."

Everything he said made her feel that he was sneering at her, and she replied:

"On the contrary, Sir, I know a great deal about looking after a little girl of Lucy's age."

It was true, she thought, because she knew exactly how Nanny had looked after her, and it annoyed her that he should be so scathing.

He was silent for a moment before he said:

"I suppose in the circumstances there is nothing I can do about it, but I very much dislike my arrangements being altered, especially without my permission."

"Nanny was not aware until this morning, that she would be unable to travel," Iola said slowly, as if she were speaking to somebody rather stupid. "The only alternative to my coming in her place would have been to send you a telegram, which she imagined might make things difficult for you if you wished to leave Southampton today."

Sir Wolfe did not speak and after a moment Iola added:

"She thought, Sir, that she was doing you a good turn."

"I dislike good turns," Sir Wolfe said almost peevishly, "they usually turn out to be the very opposite."

"Then I hope I shall prove to be the exception to the rule."

He glared at her as if he thought now there was no mistake about her impertinence. Then he said sharply:

"Put Lucy to bed. Later I will speak to you. One of the stewards will show you the way."

He walked out of the cabin without saying anything else or looking at his daughter. Iola stared after him in amazement.

He was certainly a strange and unpredictable man and, she thought, very disagreeable.

Lucy put down her doll and got up from the floor.

"Now you've made Daddy angry," she said, "but don't worry, he's often angry. I don't listen, I shut my ears."

Iola thought Lucy had an unusual relationship with her father.

"Come and help me to unpack some of my things," she said. "Then I will put you to bed. Do you always go to bed as early as this?"

"I've been ill," Lucy replied, "and they keep saying I must stay in bed. But when they are not looking, I get out and play, if I want to."

Iola wondered if she should point out that this was a mistake, but thought it much better to let it pass.

She opened the communicating-door into her own cabin and found that while they had been talking, her two trunks had been brought in and the straps undone.

It was what the footmen always did at home, and she thought, with a little jerk of fear, that it was fortunate that these servants had not opened the lid of the trunk which would have revealed her own clothes and her sable hat.

Carefully she did up the straps of her own trunk again and Lucy leant against the bed watching her.

"Why are you doing that?" she asked at last.

"I will not want this trunk while we are at sea," Iola replied.

She rose from the trunk to take off her serge cloak and her bonnet.

"Tell me about yourself," she said beguilingly.

"I think Daddy's angry because you are younger than he expected," Lucy said after a moment, "but not as angry as Aunt Isabel will be."

"Who is Aunt Isabel?" Iola asked curiously.

"She's not my real aunt," Lucy replied, "but Nanny said I was to call her one. I don't like her, and I don't like Uncle Charles, who's her husband. He's always jumping me up in the air."

Iola felt it was something she should not ask, but she was interested.

"Who else is on the yacht except you and your father, Aunt Isabel and Uncle Charles?"

"There're two other people," Lucy replied. "I can't remember their names, but they're not important. I heard Nanny say they've only been asked so that they could chap—chap—er—something like that—Daddy and Aunt Isabel."

Iola stared at the child in astonishment.

It was not the way she had expected a child of five to talk and certainly not the way she herself had talked at that age.

But she could remember absorbing a lot of what was going on round her because she had no other child of her own age to play with, and she supposed that that was what had happened with Lucy

She had spent most of her time with her Nanny and the servants, and almost automatically she listened to what they were saying, much of it, Iola was sure, unsuitable for her ears.

She did not know why, but it had never struck her that there would be a party on board the yacht.

Now she told herself that it was very unlikely that someone like Sir Wolfe Renton would leave England and all his many interests unless there was some entertainment for himself, and that was obviously where "Aunt Isabel" came in.

She began to take things out of Nanny's trunk, hanging up in the fitted wardrobe the skirts and blouses so that they would not be creased.

Then as she lifted out the plain cotton underclothes and flannel petticoats which Nanny had worn in the winter, Iola decided that underneath Nanny's uniform she would certainly wear her own lingerie.

However, as she unpacked she was thinking of the child beside her.

"Have you done any lessons?" she asked. "Can you read?"

"I can write, but I hate it!" Lucy replied. "I don't like to read. It's too difficult."

"That is a pity," Iola said, "because I have lots of stories to tell you which I have read in books, but it will not be fair unless you can tell me some too."

"Why should I tell you stories?" Lucy asked in a voice, Iola thought with amusement, that her father might have used.

"Because if you like hearing stories, then so do I," she replied.

"I can tell you stories without having to read them."

"What sort of stories?"

"Stories about the people Daddy knows. There's one man who wanted to shoot him!"

Iola looked startled.

"Why should he want to do that?"

"He said Daddy had taken his money away from him and his wife!"

Iola knew this must be servants' gossip and certainly something Lucy should not repeat.

"I think that is a dull story," she said. "I can tell you stories about dragons and fairies who dance on the lawn."

"Daddy says there are no such things as fairies. They're just lies invented by stupid people."

"I must be very stupid then," Iola said, "as there were always fairies dancing on my lawn when I was a little girl of your age. I knew exactly where they had been because early in the morning there was a ring of toadstools just where they had danced."

"I don't believe . . ." Lucy began, then she stopped. "Why did they dance?"

"Because they were happy and it was a change from flying."

"No-one can fly," Lucy said scathingly. "We haven't any wings."

"The fairies fly like birds."

Lucy considered this for a moment. Then she said:

"Perhaps what you saw were birds but because you were stupid you thought they were fairies."

This, Iola thought, was good reasoning, but she said:

"When we get to the South of France, if there is a garden full of flowers we'll go and look for the fairies. They always hide in flowers, just as elves hide in the roots of trees and the goblins burrow under the hills."

"Daddy says that is all nonsense! He took away all my books and pictures of fairies so that I wouldn't believe in a lot of lies!"

"Well, I will tell you a fairy-story before you go to sleep," Iola said. "If you do not believe it, it does not matter. I shall believe it and so it will make me happy to tell it."

"And you'll not tell Daddy, will you?" Lucy begged.

Iola realised that she was intriguing against her employer.

She told herself that she was perfectly justified in doing so. How could any man be so ridiculous as to stop a child of five from believing in fairies?

The stories Nanny had told her were, she thought, very much a part of her education.

For this child who had no mother, it was important to develop her imagination about beautiful things, things she could love, things that would mean something to her, instead of absorbing a lot of indecent gossip she had heard from the servants.

As she spoke she thought that she was doing something which was contrary to Sir Wolfe's wishes, then she told herself that she was quite certain Nanny would have done the same.

It was Nanny who had opened a whole world of imagination to her, and Iola was sure that it had moulded and fashioned her character in a way for which she could never be sufficiently grateful.

It was Nanny who had made her see beauty in so many things that she would never have noticed otherwise. It was Nanny who had made her listen to music, to find that she responded to it because it too was beautiful.

It was Nanny who had made her understand that what a person was like inside was more important than how they looked. These were the things she intended to teach Lucy.

"If you do," something warned her, "you will soon find yourself travelling back to England alone."

Then she told herself that she was just being needlessly apprehensive. Sir Wolfe did not understand children and certainly not his own.

"If I am to take Nanny's place, even for a short time,' Iola thought, 'I have to do what is best for the child, just as Nanny would have done.'

Parents who did not look after their own children were of secondary importance.

Then she told herself it was very unlikely that Sir Wolfe would think of being secondary to anybody.

There was something very authoritative about him, and something too which Iola thought could be extremely frightening.

She remembered Mr. Carter warning her that she must agree with him.

"That is what I must do," she told herself, "agree, but do what I want to do . . . my way."

Chapter Four

Iola put Lucy to bed and the child chattered all the time, saying precocious things which Iola realised had come from a gossipping old Nanny and other servants.

She was obviously an extremely intelligent little girl. At the same time, there was something rather pathetic in the fact that she was not like an ordinary child, but more like a voluble grown-up who had no companions of her own age.

She was just getting into bed when she said:

"Why do you believe in fairies?"

"Because they are exciting and beautiful little creatures who can tell us lots of precious secret things that people who live in a world of trains and machinery do not know."

Lucy considered this for a moment. Then she said:

"Fairies can't go on trains, can they?"

"I am sure they would not want to," Iola replied. "Trains are noisy and ugly, but they are convenient for getting from one place to another."

"I'd like to be able to fly," Lucy said, and Iola knew she was still thinking about fairies.

As she snuggled down against the pillows, Iola said:

"Do you not say your prayers?"

"Sometimes," Lucy said, "but when Nanny forgot I didn't remind her."

"Why not?"

"Because I don't want to talk to God. He's old and he is always spying on people, watching them to see if they do something naughty."

Iola repressed a smile.

She could not help thinking that this was rather a good description of God as far too often described in Church.

"The God I pray to is not a bit like that," she said, "but I will tell you about Him another time."

She was silent for a moment. Then Lucy said:

"I think I'd rather hear about the fairies."

"Nevertheless, I think you should say your prayers."

She thought Lucy was going to refuse, and because it was the first night she said:

"I tell you what I will do. I will say them for you, and you will see if your prayers are as nice as mine."

She knelt down by the side of the bed and put her hands together and said a prayer she had always loved:

"Matthew, Mark, Luke and John,
Bless the bed that I lie on.
Four angels to my bed,
Four angels round my head.
One to watch, and one to pray,
And two to bear my soul away."

She opened her eyes for a moment and saw that Lucy was listening intently, then she said the "Gentle Jesus" prayer that she had learnt as soon as she could speak.

"Those are nice prayers," Lucy said when Iola had finished. "Do you think there really are four angels at the top of my bed?"

"Our Guardian Angels are always with us," Iola replied, "and if we are worried about what we should do, we can ask our Guardian angels and they will answer inside our minds."

Lucy was thrilled with this.

"I can hear them speak?" she asked.

"You cannot hear them with your ears, but you can inside your head. I will tell you about it tomorrow. Go to sleep now."

She kissed Lucy and thought for a moment that the child was not going to respond, then she gave her a little peck on the cheek.

"I think I'm going to like you as my Nanny," she said, "but I don't think Daddy likes you."

That was not a very heartening thought, Iola told herself wryly as she went into the other cabin to take off her travelling-gown.

By now they were obviously away from the quay, but as they were in Southampton water and not yet in the open sea, there was only a gentle motion.

Iola put on one of Nanny's white blouses with a white skirt and clasped Nanny's belt with its silver buckle round her waist.

She glanced in the mirror and thought with a smile that her father would be very surprised if he could see her now.

Then she brushed back the little wisps of hair that had escaped onto her forehead and opened the cabin door.

There was a steward outside and as soon as she appeared he said:

"I'm to take you to the Master, Miss Dawes."

He was a middle-aged man with a decided twinkle in his eye, and before he moved ahead of her he said:

"I'm thinking you're too young to be a Nanny."

"If anybody else says that to me," Iola replied, "I think I will scream!"

The steward laughed.

"Don't let the Master hear you!"

He went ahead along the passageway and up the stairs.

When she reached the place where she had come in, and which she now realised opened into the main Saloons, she heard the noise of voices and laughter.

The steward, however, went down another passage, knocked on a door, and Iola heard Sir Wolfe answer:

"Come in!"

The door was opened for her and she walked into what she realised must be his own particular private cabin or Study.

It was austere and businesslike with a large, flat-topped desk, panelled walls, and port-holes which looked out onto the bow of the ship.

It struck her that they were directly beneath the bridge, and she thought that even sitting at his desk he could get the impression that he was navigating his own yacht.

He was writing as she entered and did not look up for a moment. She had the feeling that he was deliberately keeping her waiting, perhaps to make her feel small and insignificant.

Finally he put down his pen.

"You have already given me an explanation, Miss Dawes, as to why you are here," he said, "but I must insist that I find it extremely inconvenient when I was expecting a much older and more experienced woman to be in charge of my daughter."

Iola felt there was nothing to say to this, so she remained silent.

Sir Wolfe looked at her with his strange eyes, which seemed, she thought, to be searching for something, but she had no idea what it would be.

Then he said almost grudgingly:

"Sit down. I want to talk to you."

There was a chair in front of the desk and Iola sat on it with her back to the sea, feeling as if she was a heretic being cross-examined by the Spanish Inquisition.

"I imagine you will not be in charge of Lucy for long," Sir Wolfe began. "At the same time, I do not wish her to get into bad ways."

Iola raised her chin, feeling that this was almost insulting.

"What I mean by that is that I have made it a strict rule that the child's head should not be stuffed with a lot of fanciful falsehoods such as are doled out to most children."

"I presume by that you mean fairy-stories," Iola said.

Sir Wolfe raised his dark eye-brows.

"Why should you say that?"

"Lucy has already told me that you took her books away and told her there are no such things as fairies. I presume you have also told her there is no Father Christmas?"

"I wish my child to be brought up to hear the truth and speak the truth," Sir Wolfe said. "To start at an early age being told a lot of lies is, in my opinion, responsible for a great deal of the dishonesty which is to be found everywhere in the world today."

"You really think that fairy-stories which stimulate a child's imagination and give her an appreciation of beauty are responsible for that?" Iola asked incredulously.

"I do not intend to argue about a matter to which I have given my serious consideration," Sir Wolfe said. "I am merely informing you that you are not to tell Lucy about fairies or any other rubbish which I consider detrimental to her intelligence."

Iola was just about to argue when she remembered that Mr. Carter had told her always to agree with Sir Wolfe.

"I understand, Sir," she said.

Perhaps she overdid the meakness of her tone, for Sir Wolfe looked at her sharply.

"I mean to be obeyed in this matter."

"I do understand, Sir," Iola replied, "and I will see that no books by Shakespeare, the Brothers Grimm, or Robert Louis Stevenson are to be found in the Nursery."

She felt as she spoke that she had surprised him, and she went on:

"I was just wondering if the Bible should be excluded too."

She spoke in a deliberately innocent tone and as he looked up, she saw that his eyes were angry.

"Do you mean to be impertinent?" he enquired.

"Of course not, Sir. I was only thinking that it is very difficult to prove to a child that God actually exists. In fact, Lucy has already told me this evening that she does not like God when he is always spying on people."

Sir Wolfe's eye-brows met across the bridge of his nose.

"I gave explicit instructions to Lucy's last Nanny that she was not to teach her anything about religion but to leave that subject to a Governess."

"Lucy is to have a Governess?" Iola asked.

"Naturally!" Sir Wolfe snapped. "She has had one up until now, who came to the house three days a week to teach her reading and writing. When she is well enough she will have one permanently, but for the moment the Doctors do not wish her to over-tax her strength either mentally or physically."

His voice was more positive as he added:

"That is another thing you must remember—no long walks, no staying up late, no excitement."

"I understand, Sir."

Sir Wolfe was still glaring at her and she looked down, not aware as she did so that her eye-lashes were very long and dark against her pale skin.

"You seem to me to be far too young for this position," he said abruptly.

"I can only assure you once again that I shall look after Lucy to the best of my ability "

"That is just what I am questioning," Sir Wolfe replied, "your ability."

Iola felt that he was being unnecessarily hostile.

"I can hardly offer to leave immediately, Sir," she said, "but it will not be long, I imagine, before we reach a port."

Once again he was scowling ferociously.

"I obviously cannot ask you to leave until you can be replaced," he said. "How soon does the original Miss Dawes intend to join us?"

"As soon as she is well enough to do so."

"When will that be?"

"I am afraid I have no idea. I came away in a hurry and there was no time this morning to consult a Doctor before I left."

Sir Wolfe appeared to think for a moment, then he said:

"We must leave things as they are. Do you understand that if you are at all worried about any action you should take as regards Lucy, you will kindly consult me, not the servants!"

"I will do that, Sir."

Iola thought the interview was at an end and rose to her feet.

As she did so, the bow of the ship struck the first waves coming in from the Channel.

The ship lurched and she put out her hands to steady herself against the desk.

"One thing more," Sir Wolfe said, "I hope you are a good sailor."

"I hope so too. But like everything else we have discussed—only time will tell!"

Iola smiled as she spoke, then without waiting for his reply she moved carefully across the cabin to the door.

She had the feeling as she left him that he was looking after her with surprise.

* * *

The following morning Iola was more excited than Lucy was.

She had slept well, and although the ship was rolling quite considerably she did not feel at all sick. In fact, she ate a large breakfast and persuaded Lucy to do the same.

"I tell you what we will do," she said as the steward cleared away the dishes, "we will wrap up and go on deck to look at the waves. I have always read about the white horses but I have never seen them."

"White horses?" Lucy asked.

"That is what they call the waves when they are breaking, and the white foam looks like horses riding over the green water."

Lucy clapped her hands together.

"That sounds fun! Let's go and look."

Iola searched in a wardrobe to find a little white fur coat and white woollen leggings in which she could dress Lucy.

Then she went to her own cabin and knew that in Nanny's serge cape she would be cold, very cold.

She remembered, however, that she had a jacket lined with ermine which she sometimes wore at home.

She unpacked it quickly and slipped it over her white blouse, then put the serge cape over it.

"If I get a cold," she told herself, "Sir Wolfe will think I am more of a nuisance than he does already."

She put on Nanny's little black bonnet; then, knowing her ears would be cold, she tied a large white handkerchief over her head and knotted it under her chin.

Although she looked strange she thought that no-one would notice her.

Holding Lucy's gloved hand in hers, they walked up the stairs. A steward saw them and exclaimed:

"You're not going out in this weather?"

"It is cold, but a breath of air will do us both good," Iola answered.

"If you ask me, that's a sensible way of looking at things," he replied.

He was a youngish man and Iola did not miss the admiration in his eyes as he looked at her.

He opened the door for them, saying:

"Now you be careful not to be blown away. If you keep on this side of the ship, it's more to leeward."

"That is just what I was going to ask you," Iola said. "We will do as you say."

Holding on tightly to Lucy, Iola staggered a little way down the deck, gradually getting her balance until without going right out into the wind they could see the waves breaking over the bow.

"Show me the white horses!" Lucy cried.

Iola pointed out the waves breaking all round them and over the deck as the yacht forged ahead.

Occasional drops of spray touched her cheek and she thought it was exhilarating, and she was sure it was better for Lucy than being cooped up down below in the airless cabin.

"It is very lovely!" Iola said almost as if she was speaking to herself. "I know now why sailors believe in mermaids that live beneath the oceans."

"Mermaids?" Lucy asked.

"Lovely laides with fish-tails instead of legs," Iola explained.

Lucy was intrigued and they sat down watching the sea while Iola told her about the mermaids, with their long hair falling over their shoulders, their sweet voices that sometimes made the sailors who listened to them drive their ships upon the rocks.

It was only as Lucy asked for more that she remembered that mermaids undoubtedly came into the same category as fairies, dragons, and other imaginary creatures which Sir Wolfe described as nonsensical lies.

As she thought of him it was almost as if she conjured him up, for he came walking along the deck towards them, looking, she thought, exceedingly handsome in a yachting-cap, his heavy overcoat open to show his yachting-jacket with its brass buttons underneath.

"I am surprised to see you here," he said sharply when he reached them. "I should have thought it was too cold for Lucy."

"I'm not cold, Daddy," Lucy said before Iola could speak. "We came out to see the white horses."

"You must not catch a chill," Sir Wolfe said.

"She is well wrapped up," Iola pleaded.

"I'm quite all right," Lucy cried. "Do go away, Daddy. I want Nanny to go on telling me about the mermaids."

Iola drew in her breath as she saw Sir Wolfe's lips tighten.

She thought he was going to say something scathing about her not obeying his orders. Instead he merely walked away and Lucy said with a sigh of relief:

"Now he's gone, go on with your story, or tell me another one. I want to see a mermaid."

Because the sea became very much rougher for the next two days, Iola and Lucy really were confined to their cabins.

She tried to obey Sir Wolfe's orders and not tell Lucy fairy-stories, but they were in fact the only type of tales which came to her mind and which she thought were suitable for a five-year-old.

So, sooner or later she always slipped back into telling a story that Nanny had told her, or answering Lucy's questions in a manner which made her demand more, of which she was quite certain Sir Wolfe would not approve.

"His whole idea of how to bring up a child is ridiculous!" she told herself. "I could understand it if Lucy were a boy, but as she is a girl, what does it matter if everything she learns is not academically correct?"

She was surprised that neither Sir Wolfe nor any member of the party came to see Lucy, until she learnt from the steward that the ladies were sea-sick and the men, with the exception of Sir Wolfe, were finding it easier to drink than to eat.

"We'll soon be out of it, Nanny," he said reassuringly.

The staff had all begun to call her Nanny but she thought the way they said it made it more of an endearment than in deference to her status.

She knew the stewards admired her and were far more attentive than they had ever been to any real Nanny. The Chief Steward even offered her a glass of wine with her supper, which she thought it wise to refuse.

Fortunately, she discovered that there was a Library on board, and one of the stewards brought her a selection of books and changed them when she asked him for new ones.

The food was delicious, but with no-one to talk to except Lucy, Iola found it hard to keep from thinking of her own problem of what she should do in the future.

Obviously Sir Wolfe, once he realised that Nanny was not going to join them, would insist on engaging an older Nurse for Lucy.

Then she would have to make up her mind whether to return to England or try to get some sort of employment in France.

She had a feeling that this might be very difficult unless she enlisted the help of Sir Wolfe, which was the last thing she would think of doing.

"It is no use worrying," she told herself. "I have just got to wait and see what happens."

In other words, she thought with a smile, she was back to "time will tell."

By the time they had passed through the Bay of Biscay and the sea grew calmer, there was sunshine coming through the grey clouds and Lucy was showing her affection in a dozen different ways, being easier to control with every hour that passed.

"I like you, I like you very much!" she said to Iola the fourth night she had been on board.

"And I love you," Iola replied.

Lucy put her head on one side before she said:

"I love you too, but Daddy said I am not to talk about love. It is a useless emotion which makes people behave stupidly."

"That is not true!" Iola said indignantly. "Love is something we all feel and it is very important that we should. You must have been mistaken in what your father said. He loves you as you love him."

"Daddy loves nobody but himself!" Lucy contradicted. "I heard Nanny say so, and she said that my mother didn't love him and that's why he says all loving is wrong."

This was certainly a new aspect of the subject, Iola thought, but she knew she should not encourage Lucy to talk in such a way.

Instead she said:

"I will tell you a story about a little girl who had a dog she loved and who, because he loved her so much, saved her life."

"Tell me, tell me!" Lucy cried, and the uncomfortable moment was forgotten.

They were just finishing the story when a steward knocked at the door and came in to say:

"You're to take Miss Lucy up to the Saloon at tea-time. Now that Her Ladyship's found her 'sea-legs,' she wants to see her."

"What are 'sea-legs'?" Lucy asked.

"It's what you and Nanny have had ever since

we started," the steward answered, "and, I expect, very pretty legs too!"

He winked at Iola before he left the cabin, and she wondered with amusement what her father would say if he could hear the familiar way the staff talked to her because they treated her as one of themselves.

She changed Lucy's gown for one of the smarter ones which hung in the wardrobe, put on her white silk socks and her red slippers, tied a red bow of ribbon on each side of her head, and took her up to the Saloon.

Ever since she had heard about Lady Isabel she had been extremely curious to see what she looked like, wondering what sort of women Sir Wolfe would find attractive.

The moment she entered the Saloon she admitted that he had extremely good taste.

Lady Isabel was beautiful. Her figure, with a tiny pulled-in waist, her red-gold hair, and the imperious manner in which she carried herself made Iola think she might have stepped straight out of a painting by Sargent.

She was reclining on a sofa of green velvet and Iola was certain she was well aware that its silk cushions of the same colour made a perfect background for her white skin and large gentian-blue eyes.

"Dearest Lucy, how nice to see you!" she exclaimed. "Good-afternoon, Nanny! I have been hearing from Sir Wolfe that your charge is better in health. That is excellent news!"

"I think the sea-air has done her good, My Lady," Iola replied.

"Come and talk to me, dearest child," Lady Isabel said to Lucy, patting the sofa beside her.

"What can we talk about that's interesting?" Lucy asked, moving across the Saloon slowly.

Lady Isabel laughed.

"Anything. Would you like me to tell you what a

lovely ship I think this is, and how kind it was of your dear Daddy to ask me to sail in it with you?"

Her voice was so honey-sweet that Iola was not surprised to realise that Sir Wolfe had entered the cabin behind them, and although she had not been aware of his presence, Lady Isabel had.

Sir Wolfe walked towards the sofa, and although Iola could not see his eyes, she was quite certain that they were full of admiration for the picture Lady Isabel made with Lucy standing beside her.

"Dear Wolfe!" she said, holding out her hand in an almost theatrical gesture. "I wish I could express how happy I am to be here with you and your adorable little daughter."

Iola wondered uncomfortably whether she was expected to stay or to go, and, telling herself that if she was wanted Sir Wolfe would send for her, she moved a few steps backwards towards the door.

As she reached it, Lucy realised her intention and said:

"I want to go with Nanny. She has lots of interesting things to tell me."

"I have things to tell you too," Lady Isabel said.

She put her arm round Lucy as she spoke, and Iola, anticipating that the child was going to be difficult, did not leave the Saloon.

Instead she stood at the door waiting.

"Shall I tell you one of the nursery-rhymes I knew when I was a little girl?" Lady Isabel asked.

"I know all the nursery-rhymes," Lucy replied. "I learnt them years and years ago!"

"Then what are you learning now?" Lady Isabel asked.

"Nanny tells me stories, very exciting ones," Lucy said, "and I believe everything she tells me—everything!"

She looked defiantly at her father as she spoke, and as if he realised that Lucy was being deliberately provocative, he glanced at Iola before he said:

"I think you had better go below now. I expect it is time you had your tea."

"I suppose you're sending me away because you want to talk to Aunt Isabel all alone," Lucy said. "Well, I'd rather be with Nanny, she's much more fun."

She tossed her head as she spoke and ran across the Saloon to Iola.

She put her hand in hers and said:

"Come on, Nanny! It's terribly boring up here. It always is!"

Iola felt there was nothing she could say or do. She merely opened the door for Lucy and followed her out of the Saloon.

If she could have stayed she would not have been surprised by what was said. In fact, she would have expected it.

"Really, Wolfe!" Lady Isabel remarked. "I do not think that theatrical-looking young woman is doing Lucy any good."

"Theatrical?" Sir Wolfe questioned.

"I would not be surprised if that was mascara on her eye-lashes," Lady Isabel said, "or else she dyes her hair. I cannot believe any woman was born with fair hair and dark eye-lashes—a most unnatural combination!"

"I never thought of it."

"She is too pretty, too young, and obviously far too ignorant to be with a clever child like Lucy. You must get rid of her immediately we reach Monte Carlo."

"That is not a very practical idea," Sir Wolfe remarked, "considering it will be difficult to find somebody else so quickly."

"I will find you someone," Lady Isabel said. "You obviously cannot allow her to stay."

There was a determination in her voice that Sir Wolfe did not miss.

* * *

The Villa was everything that Iola had expected, only much more so.

Situated behind Monte Carlo high up in the hills, the view was fantastic, the garden a dream of delight.

As soon as the yacht was moored in the harbour beneath the town of Monte Carlo, she thought that she had stepped into a fairy-land she had always wished to see.

She had always believed that the description of the blue of the Mediterranean must be exaggerated, but she found it really was the blue of the Madonna's robe, and the mountains behind the Principality were silhouetted against the blue sky and the sun seemed more golden than any sunshine she had seen before.

"It is lovely! Lovely!" she exclaimed as she and Lucy stood on deck and watched the yacht move into the harbour. "Oh, I am so glad to be here! So glad I came!"

She spoke with a lilt in her voice, then started as Sir Wolfe said:

"I hope Lucy shares your enthusiasm and shows her happiness by being better behaved in the future than she has been up-to-date."

"My last Nanny always said I was just like you," Lucy said, "and you aren't always well behaved, Daddy."

"You must not talk to your father like that," Iola remonstrated in a low voice.

"Why not?" Lucy enquired. "He says I'm always to speak the truth, and it is the truth."

Iola could not help a little laugh escaping from her lips. Then as two dimples appeared in her cheeks, she looked at Sir Wolfe and found to her surprise that he was smiling too.

"Hoist by my own petard!" he said. "Oh well, I suppose you are thinking: 'Out of the mouths of babes and sucklings came forth wisdom,' even if you are too polite to say so!"

"I try not to think impolitely either," Iola replied.

"I am relieved to hear that," Sir Wolfe answered, but he was smiling as he walked away from them.

At the Villa Iola found that she and Lucy were allotted rooms at the other end of the building from those occupied by Sir Wolfe and his guests.

Although there had only been four guests on board, she learnt from Mr. Carter, who, with Harold, was the only servant to come with them from the yacht, that there would be a lot more people joining them as soon as they settled in.

"The other ladies and gentlemen," he told Iola, "preferred to come over-land."

"Perhaps their decision was wise," Iola replied. "After all, Lady Isabel and Sir Wolfe's other guests spent most of the time in their cabins."

Mr. Carter laughed.

"Her Ladyship wasn't going to let the Master out of her sight! There'll be some real beauties staying with us this week. You have a look at them, if you gets the chance."

"I will," Iola promised.

But she told herself, now that they had arrived, that she was not really interested.

She took Lucy out to explore the garden and found it was an enchantment that left her breathless.

The beauty of the bougainvillaea growing over the walls, the mimosa trees just coming into flower, the pale pink geraniums that appeared to be everywhere, were all so vivid and so lovely that she wished she were an artist and could paint everything she saw.

Sir Wolfe had not built the Villa. Its previous owner had lived there for many years after his retirement and had devoted himself to making it one of the most outstanding gardens on the whole Riviera.

There were little cascades of water falling into exquisitely carved stone basins, and there were stone steps and paths which twisted and turned to show vistas of the sea or small secretive groves that one felt had never been discovered before.

Even Lucy was awed by it all.

"I think, although we'll not tell Daddy, that the fairies would like to live in a garden like this," she said to Iola in a whisper.

"I am sure they do live here," Iola replied.

She felt it was impossible to think anything else because for her it was definitely fairy-land, and as she thought of it she wondered if Sir Wolfe was in fact the wicked ogre who would send her away from it.

"I shall be more careful to do what he wants," she told herself. "I will agree to everything he says. In fact, I would agree with the Devil himself if I could stay in this little Paradise!"

It was obvious that she and Lucy had the garden entirely to themselves.

Laughing, usually with champagne-glasses in their hands, Sir Wolfe's party would wander out onto the terrace outside the large Drawing-Room which had French windows from where there was the best view, but otherwise they seldom seemed to encroach anywhere and Iola spent every moment she could in the garden either with Lucy or alone.

She went out at night after her supper, knowing that as soon as dinner was finished Sir Wolfe and his friends would drive into Monte Carlo to the Casino.

She wondered if he was a gambler, but she felt that having earned his money the hard way, he would resent it being thrown away on the green baize tables depending not on intelligence but on the turn of a card.

She thought she really knew nothing about him except that he was immensely rich and had some very foolish ideas about bringing up a child.

Nevertheless, though she seldom saw him, his personality seemed to have impressed itself on the Villa, on the servants, and on her.

It was difficult to escape from thinking about him.

She could understand that Lady Isabel wished to keep him interested in her, or was it a deep affection?

Iola had seen Lady Isabel's husband, Captain Charles Unwin, walking round the deck.

He looked a rather stupid man with a fair moustache, a typical Officer in the Brigade of Guards, Iola thought, with a rather loud laugh, but she had seen too little of him to be able to judge at all clearly what he was like.

She had the idea, however, that he was content for his wife to be favoured by Sir Wolfe simply because he was so rich.

"It is what one might expect," she told herself, "in the glittering world of those who, like the King, seek only pleasure for themselves and the good things of life."

She had read about the enormous pheasant-shoots that were arranged for the King and his friends and the Balls that were given at places like Warwick Castle, Chatsworth, and Wentworth Woodhouse.

She had also read a little in the past about the gaiety of Monte Carlo.

She wondered, now that she was here, whether she would have a chance to see the actresses with their hats covered with ospreys and wearing their sensational jewels, or have a glimpse of the huge dinner-parties that were given by the Russian Princes and of course men as rich as Sir Wolfe.

'It is a fascinating world to which I shall never belong,' she thought.

Then she remembered that if she was Lady Stoneham, the doors would be open to her and she would accompany her husband to Court functions.

"I am much happier as I am," she told herself gaily.

Having finished her supper, she walked out through the open window into the garden.

Lucy was fast asleep; in fact she had slept well ever since they had arrived and Iola had no reason to worry about her until the morning.

She walked across the grass, finding now that it was dark there was a chill in the air which she learnt could be treacherous.

She had in fact picked up a warm shawl before she had left the Nursery.

She put it round her shoulders and crossed it over her breast, knowing she was not in the least cold but excited because the stars were coming out overhead and there was a pale moon shimmering on the sea, turning it to silver.

She walked on until she found herself negotiating one of the twisting little paths which led between the banks of flowers.

She was deep in her thoughts when she was suddenly conscious of voices, then the fragrance of cigar-smoke, and she stopped still.

She was not quite certain from which direction the voices came, but she had no wish to be seen.

Then she heard a man say:

"Well, I suppose we had better join the others, although I am not keen on gambling tonight. I have lost a bomb already this week."

The other man laughed.

"Like our host, you can afford it!"

"Not so easily," the first man replied.

"That reminds me," the first one said, "I think Charles is up to his tricks again."

"Do you mean where Renton is concerned?"

"Who else?"

"Yes, of course; now that you mention it, it is obvious that Renton is a little smitten."

"I suppose so. It is difficult to tell. He is a strange person, but we are all aware what Isabel is like!"

"Once bitten, twice shy, eh, George? We have all been a victim at one time or another."

"That is true, but I don't like to remember it now."

"Do you intend to warn Renton?"

"Why should I? He is old enough and rich enough to take care of himself. It just annoys me that Charles should always get away with it. Personally I always think it pays to mind one's own business."

"I agree with you, but Renton has been pretty good to me, one way or another. He let me in on that last issue of his and I made quite a killing."

"Then you intend to give him a hint?"

There was silence for a moment.

"No. I think not. He might take it the wrong way, and Isabel, as we both know, has a tongue like an asp!"

"You never spoke a truer word! Come on, let's go into Monte. And if you take my advice, you will let sleeping dogs lie."

"That is what I intend to do."

The two men who had been talking rose and Iola could hear their footsteps on the path until they must have reached the grass.

She was thinking over what she had heard. It had been a strange conversation and she could not quite understand what it meant.

She supposed that Captain Charles, Lady Isabel's husband, was planning to get money out of Sir Wolfe in some way or other, but how? And why did his friends consider warning Sir Wolfe, even though they were too cautious to do so?

It was all very mysterious and she found herself thinking about it all the time she walked back to the house, and later when she found it hard to sleep.

The following morning Lucy and Iola were in the garden early and quite unexpectedly Sir Wolfe joined them.

"Good-morning, Lucy!" he said, and nodded to Iola as she said:

"Good-morning, Sir!"

"Hello, Daddy," Lucy said. "I've counted twenty-two different flowers. How many can you count?"

"I have no idea," Sir Wolfe answered.

Then he said to Iola in a surprisingly pleasant voice:

"Is this a new sort of game?"

"I suppose it would sound better if I said it was botany combined with arithmetic," Iola replied without thinking.

"It's a game," Lucy said indignantly, "and one day when I can beat Nanny I'm going to win a prize."

"That is bribery and corruption," Sir Wolfe said, his eyes twinkling.

"On the contrary, Sir, it is a reward for honest endeavour," Iola retorted.

Lucy looked from one to the other; then, naturally not understanding the conversation, she ran across the lawn crying:

"I'm going to catch a butterfly!"

Sir Wolfe followed her with his eyes.

"She is obviously better."

"Much. She eats well and sleeps well."

"I suppose I should apologise for doubting your capabilities," Sir Wolfe said.

"No, of course not," Iola replied, "anyone would have felt the same, and I shall always be extremely grateful, Sir, for having the chance to come here."

"You certainly look happier," he said.

She looked at him in astonishment.

"Happier?" she repeated.

"I sensed, and I am seldom wrong when I follow my instinct, that something had recently upset you when you came aboard the yacht. There was undoubtedly a stricken expression in your eyes."

Iola was still.

She had the impulse to tell him the truth, to admit that Nanny was dead and she would never be joining them as he was expecting.

Then she told herself that it would be a very stupid thing to do.

However pleased he might be about the improvement in Lucy, she would be giving him the chance to be rid of her as soon as he could find a replacement.

While he was satisfied that it was only a temporary arrangement, she could stay longer, very much longer.

She looked up at him and found his strange eyes looking at her.

"Well?" he asked. "Have you made up your mind?"

"About . . . what?"

"Whatever was troubling you."

"How . . . how do you know there is . . . anything? I do not . . . understand what you are saying."

Sir Wolfe's lips twisted in a smile.

"Perhaps I should warn you that I have the faculty, although I do not often use it, of knowing intuitively what people are thinking and feeling. I find it something very easy to do where you are concerned."

"Then please . . . do not do it!" Iola said quickly. "It is an . . . intrusion and . . . something which . . . frightens me."

"It could only do that if you had something to hide."

Iola drew in her breath.

She was looking across the garden at Lucy and for the moment she did not see her. She was seeing first Lord Stoneham's face, then Nanny's.

"Have you anything to hide?" Sir Wolfe asked insistently.

Iola knew suddenly that she could not answer him, could not let him ask her any more questions.

She was afraid not only of his questions but of him.

She felt as though he was overpowering her, compelling her to reveal the truth . . . the truth by which he set so much store.

She gave a little sound that was half a cry.

"I must go to Lucy," she said, and ran away from him across the lawn.

Chapter Five

"Look what I've brought you, Miss Lucy!"

Harold handed Lucy a little red paper windmill such as street vendors sold at every seaside resort.

Lucy gave a cry of delight.

"It's pretty!"

"When you run, it'll turn round and round," Harold said, "and if there's a wind it'll go quicker still."

Iola smiled.

"That was kind of you, Harold. We are driving up to La Turbie today and we will take it with us in the carriage. I am sure it will turn very fast."

Then as Lucy ran round the room watching her windmill twirl, Iola said:

"That is the second present you have given Miss Lucy this week. You must not spend your money on her."

"That's all right," Harold answered, "I'm feeling rich. Lord Rothschild left yesterday.

"Lord Rothschild?" Iola exclaimed. "He was staying here? I wish I had known."

"Why?" Harold enquired.

"I have heard so much about him that I would have liked to see him."

"He wasn't much to look at," Harold said, "but

he gave Mr. Mayhew a sum of money to be divided amongst the staff, and I got my share."

Mr. Mayhew was Sir Wolfe's secretary, and he was in fact the man who had interviewed Nanny for the post about which she had been so excited.

Iola had been apprehensive when she heard he had arrived, in case he was suspicious about her and cross-examined her as to why she had taken Nanny's place.

But obviously Sir Wolfe had not complained, and when Mr. Mayhew had been in the Villa for three days and had not sent for her, she heaved a sigh of relief and forgot about him.

But yesterday she had been brave enough to ask him if it would be possible for her to take Lucy driving.

Iola was not only thinking of Lucy's health and that a change of scene would be interesting for her, she was also thinking of herself.

She longed to see more of Monte Carlo, and, having read the history of the Principality, she was anxious to inspect the Roman ruins which she knew were still in existence at La Turbie.

"Of course you may take the child driving," Mr. Mayhew said. "I cannot think why you did not ask for the carriage before now."

"There was no need," Iola explained, not wishing to admit that she had been avoiding him. "There has been plenty to explore in the garden."

"Sir Wolfe has told me how improved in health Lucy seems to be," Mr. Mayhew said. "I am sure we can be grateful to you on that account."

"I hope so," Iola answered, and felt a little nervous in case he should ask about Nanny.

He was obviously busy and she hurried away, glad that he had promised they could have a carriage whenever they wished.

"It is exciting, Lucy!" Iola said when she got back to the Nursery. "We can drive to all the places that are mentioned in the Guide-Book. There are a lot of them."

"And you will tell me stories about every one?" Lucy questioned.

"I am sure I will be able to do that," Iola said with a smile, thinking that if there was not a story she would invent one.

She liked to think that she was doing for Lucy what Nanny had done for her, opening her mind to so many different possibilities, although she was sure Lucy was far more intelligent than she had been at that age.

She found it rather fascinating to know that she could evoke a new train of thought in Lucy's mind and to know from the questions she asked and the way she would return to a subject that she had stimulated her imagination.

Whatever Sir Wolfe might say, she still considered this an extremely important part of a child's education.

"What would we be without our imaginations?" she asked herself. "Nothing but an accumulation of dry facts without any life in them!"

She felt she wanted to say something like that to Lucy's father, but knew she would be too shy to do so. Also, as Mr. Carter had warned her from the very beginning, it was a mistake to argue with him.

'He thinks he knows everything,' she thought, 'but he is mistaken. I am sure there are things I can tell him of which he has no idea whatsoever.'

It was a fascinating thought, because every day she found new examples of Sir Wolfe's active and inventive brain.

On the yacht she had been shown many gadgets that he had personally invented, and she had learnt that he had in fact practically designed the whole vessel himself.

In the Villa there were comforts big and small which she was sure were different from anything to be found in other houses, and the whole place was a model of efficiency and well-thought-out organisation.

The servants were French, and, apart from Mr. Mayhew, the only personal staff that Sir Wolfe brought with him were his valet Carter, and Harold, who was assistant valet and personal footman.

There were of course, Iola learnt, a large number of visiting servants who were mostly English.

No fashionable lady would think of travelling without her lady's-maid, nor a gentleman without his valet, and as these all had to be catered for, almost as assiduously as their Masters and Mistresses, there appeared to be an army of servants to see to the comfort of the visitors both upstairs and down.

Because she was content with the beauty of the garden, the books which she found Harold could bring up from the Library, and with Lucy herself, Iola was not really interested in what went on in the rest of the Villa and she seldom asked who the guests were.

Some came for only a night or two, some stayed longer. Some, like Lady Isabel and her husband, appeared to be permanent.

Because she was disappointed at missing Lord Rothschild, she asked:

"Who else of any importance is staying at the moment?"

"They are all that," Harold said with a grin, "or they think they are!"

He was only nineteen and Iola thought that he was sometimes lonely amongst all the foreigners, which was why he came to the Nursery bringing Lucy presents and talking to her.

She had learnt that he had lost his mother the previous year, and as his father was also dead he had no home. She felt sorry for him, feeling that for him, like herself, the world was a big place in which to feel helpless and insignificant.

"Tell me the names," she said now, knowing that to show her interest would please Harold.

He reeled off a long list of distinguished people, some of whom were leaving on the afternoon train.

"Captain Unwin's going too," he said.

Iola looked surprised.

"Going?" she asked.

"Only for the night, and you can bet Her Ladyship'll make the most of it."

Iola did not reply and Harold went on:

"She's got her claws well and truly into the Master. She was seething last night because she thought he was talking too long to the Duchess."

Iola felt she should not encourage Harold to talk of his Master's guests in such a way. At the same time, despite herself she was interested in anything that concerned Lady Isabel.

She knew the beautiful woman disliked her.

Only yesterday afternoon when she and Lucy had been playing in the garden Lady Isabel had seen them and had walked slowly across the lawn with her sunshade held over her head, to say:

"So you are still here, Nanny! I am surprised!"

"Yes, I am still here, My Lady," Iola said quietly.

"I cannot think that you are really suited to Nursery life," Lady Isabel went on.

There was no doubt of the hostility that was in her voice and in her eyes.

"I find it very agreeable, My Lady," Iola replied.

"I have heard of a much older and more experienced woman whom I shall recommand to Sir Wolfe, and I suggest that in your own interests you start looking for another post."

"How kind of you to be so considerate," Iola said, making no effort to hide the sarcasm in her voice.

"I think the Nanny of whom I have heard will be able to take over within a week or so, perhaps sooner," Lady Isabel said.

Without waiting for Iola to reply, she walked away, the train of her expensive gown moving over the green grass, making her look exceedingly elegant.

"It is ridiculous that she should be jealous of someone she considers only a servant," Iola told herself.

But when she looked in the mirror she knew that the warm air, the sunshine, and the excellent food at the Villa had improved her looks as well as Lucy's.

There was certainly a glow on her face that had not been there before, and she knew that Sir Wolfe was right when he said the stricken look had gone from her eyes and most of the anxiety from her face.

She had been so frightened at running away, so tense and so desperately shocked by Nanny's death, that when she had arrived at Southampton it was not surprising that what she had been feeling had shown in her face.

Now as the days passed she began to feel secure, and she had moments of almost spiritual happiness because everything round her was so lovely.

All the servants were extremely kind to her, especially the French maids when they found she could speak to them fluently in their own language.

In fact the only fly in the ointment was Lady Isabel, and Iola thought of what Harold had said.

Because she was mildly curious, she asked:

"Why is Captain Unwin going away?"

"He says he has business in Nice," Harold answered, "but Mr. Carter says he's never done a day's work in his life. He's not a tipper, I can tell you that! We never get a sixpence out of him!"

It struck Iola that this was what the gentlemen she had heard talking in the garden had been discussing.

She clearly remembered one saying: "I think Charles is up to his tricks again."

What tricks? And why should they take him to Nice?

Harold giggled.

"They say absence makes the heart grow fonder," he said, "But where Her Ladyship's concerned, all the fondness that's going is for the Master. She'll make the very most of having him alone."

Something in the way Harold spoke made Iola feel uncomfortable.

She hated listening to innuendoes about the behaviour of Sir Wolfe's guests, thinking that whatever they did it should not encroach on the atmosphere in the Nursery.

As Lucy was far too precocious, Iola was anxious that nothing be said in front of her which might arouse her curiosity about things which should certainly not concern her.

Quickly now she changed the subject.

"Thank you again for the lovely present you brought for Lucy," she said. "After she has been out in the carriage, she will be able to tell you what happens when the wind catches it."

"I'm glad she likes it," Harold replied.

He went from the Nursery, and Iola found herself thinking of what he had said about Captain Charles going to Nice and Lady Isabel "making the most of it."

Despite every resolution to erase it from her mind, all the time they were driving up the twisting road which zig-zagged above Monte Carlo towards La Turbie, the question of what Captain Charles intended and how it concerned what the gentlemen had called "his tricks" was incessantly in her mind.

When they reached La Turbie, Lucy was fascinated by the Roman pillars which stood sentinel on a rock from which there was a fantastic view of the whole coast-line.

But after she had listened to Iola telling her about the Romans and their buildings which had survived for so many centuries, she grew bored and ran about, letting her windmill blow in the wind.

The view was so lovely that Iola was happy to stand there feeling that she must capture it forever in her mind.

The azure blue of the sea shading to emerald green, then fading to where the rough waves lapped against the grey rocks was enthralling.

So was the town of Monte Carlo below them, verdant Cap Ferrat jutting out into the sea, and the distant islands looking luminous in the heat of the afternoon sun.

She awoke from a kind of reverie with a start to realise that Lucy was talking to two Frenchmen who had climbed up the rock without her being aware of it.

She was showing them her windmill and Iola hurried towards her.

"*Bonjour, Messieurs,*" she said politely; then to Lucy:

"Come along, dearest, it is time for us to go home. As the horses have to go slowly down the hill it will take us some time."

"This is a very pretty young lady," one of the Frenchmen said. "I think she is the daughter of the very rich Sir Renton, is she not?"

"Yes, Sir Wolfe Renton," Iola corrected him.

Pulling Lucy with her, she started down the rough path which led to where they had left the carriage in the centre of the small village below them.

As they went, Lucy chattering about her windmill, she was aware that the two men were following them.

She did not know why, but she felt a little uncomfortable that they should be doing so and thought that perhaps she should not have admitted that Lucy was Sir Wolfe's daughter.

But she told herself it would have been foolish to lie and rude not to answer.

Anyway, if they were so curious, they could have asked the coachman or the footman, who were waiting for them by the extremely smart open Victoria in which they had travelled up the hill.

They climbed into it and as the horses started off Iola saw that the two Frenchmen were talking to another man who was standing at one of the strange little houses that were built right into the rock at the side of the road.

'It is strange,' she thought, 'that they should know Sir Wolfe's name.'

Then she thought that as his Villa was so large and conspicuous, it was not really surprising that visitors to the Principality should be inquisitive as to who was the owner.

"It is one of the penalties of being rich," she told herself with a smile, and thought that as things were at the moment, that was something that would never trouble her.

Lucy was in good spirits all the way home.

The windmill had made her curious about the speed of different things, and she asked Iola how fast horses went, what was the speed of a train, and whether a horse galloping very quickly would go faster than a train. And was a yacht like her father's as fast as a big ship like the ones in which he travelled to America?

Iola had to confess that she did not know the answers to all the questions.

"You must ask your father," she said, "I am sure he would be able to tell you."

"He's always too busy!" Lucy said scornfully.

"I am sure he is never too busy if you ask him questions which will show him that you are clever," Iola said. "Anyway, try. Perhaps we will see him when we get home."

Because she thought it would be a good idea to show Sir Wolfe that Lucy was really interested in things of which he would approve, she asked the Butler when they stepped out at the Villa:

"Is Sir Wolfe in?"

"The Master's in the Drawing-Room, *M'mselle,*" he replied in French.

"Perhaps you would ask him if he would like to see Miss Lucy after tea."

The Butler went to do her bidding and Iola waited in the Hall.

"The Master said Miss Lucy can come in now," he answered on his return.

Iola pushed the child towards the door.

"Ask your father the questions you have just asked me," she said. "I am sure he will give you the answers."

Lucy was never shy.

Looking exceedingly pretty in her pink frilled dress with a light coat of the same colour and a muslin hat which framed her face like a halo, she ran into the Drawing-Room still carrying her windmill.

Iola did not follow her, she stood just outside the open door.

"Hello, Lucy!" she heard Sir Wolfe say in his deep voice.

"How sweet you look, dearest child! Just like a little rose-bud!"

Iola recognised the effusive sweetness, which she was sure was entirely superficial, of Lady Isabel.

"Nanny said I was to ask you," Lucy was saying, "that if there was a race between a train and a horse, who would win?"

"That is certainly a difficult question," Sir Wolfe replied. "It of course depends on both the horse and the train. I think one of my race-horses would certainly beat the trains you see coming slowly along beside the sea."

"I've not seen them," Lucy said. "Are they very slow, like snails?"

"Not quite as slow as that," Sir Wolfe said. "You must tell Nanny to take you to the station and watch them arrive."

"I'll do that," Lucy said. "Perhaps I'll race one myself. I can run very, very fast."

"I am sure you can," Lady Isabel said, "because you are clever like your father. Do you know, Lucy, he is the cleverest man I have ever met in my life, and perhaps the cleverest man in the world."

"Are you the cleverest man in the world, Daddy?" Lucy asked.

"I hope so," Sir Wolfe laughed, "and I would like you to be the cleverest woman."

Lucy obviously considered this for a moment, then she said:

"Nanny says it's more important to be kind and good than to be clever, and people who think they have beautiful faces are really ugly unless their hearts are beautiful too."

Iola thought with amusement that Lucy was quoting almost word for word what Nanny had told her when she was a child.

"Nanny is quite right," he said, "and so I hope, Lucy, that your heart is beautiful."

"I am sure it is," Lady Isabel said before Lucy could speak, "and I hope my heart is beautiful too."

"I don't think it can be," Lucy said in what Iola knew was her thinking voice, "because Harold said you've got your claws into Daddy. Claws are what dangerous wild animals have, like bears and tigers!"

There was a little gasp from Lady Isabel, and Sir Wolfe said:

"That is quite enough, Lucy! Run away and have your tea."

Lucy obeyed him, holding up her windmill and running across the Drawing-Room to the door.

When she came out into the Hall where Iola was waiting for her, she heard Lady Isabel say:

"I have told you before, Wolfe, that the sooner you get rid of that young woman, the better. She has obviously been talking to the servants in front of the child and this is completely unforgivable!"

Iola thought very much the same thing. With her cheeks burning she took Lucy to the Nursery.

It was no use saying to Lucy that she should not have repeated what she had heard, because she should not have heard it in the first place.

When Iola thought how careful she had been to prevent from repeating the servants' gossip as she had done when she first arrived in the yacht, it was infuriating to think that Sir Wolfe would imagine it was she who was gossipping.

"I'd no idea she was listening to Harold," she told herself miserably.

She felt that Lady Isabel had won and she would doubtless find herself leaving the Villa very shortly.

It brought back all her fears for the future and the terrifying question of what she should do.

She was quite sure it was too soon to go back home in the hope that Lord Stoneham would have forgotten about her.

She was very quiet when she put Lucy to bed, and the child, sensing that something was wrong, asked:

"Are you angry, Nanny?"

"No, except that you were rude to Lady Isabel. You are old enough, Lucy, to know you should not have repeated what Harold said, which was not meant for your ears."

"Harold did say it, and I hate Aunt Isabel! She puts on a different voice when she speaks to me in front of Daddy to the one she uses at other times."

"Perhaps she does," Iola admitted, "but it is one of the things you must not say."

"Why not? It's the truth and Daddy likes the truth."

"But you repeated something that Harold had said which he should not have said, and now Daddy will be angry not with you but with Harold."

"I like Harold. He's kind and he brings me presents."

"Yes, I know. That is why you should not have repeated what he said. Perhaps now he will be sent away."

"I'll tell Daddy it was not his fault."

Iola did not answer, and after a moment Lucy asked:

"Do you really think Daddy will send Harold away?"

"He might. He might send me away as well."

Lucy gave a little cry.

"No, Nanny! No! You're not to go away. I'll not let you. I'll not have one of those horrid old Nannies again who never told me stories, but kept ordering me to be quiet and play with my dolls."

Iola put her arms round the little girl and held her close.

There was no question of Lucy not kissing her good-night, as she hugged her several times a day in an excess of affection.

Iola had come to the conclusion some time ago that what the child was lacking was love.

Her father was undemonstrative where she was concerned, and when Lucy had been naughty in the past it was largely because she wanted attention, not the sort the servants gave her but from somebody who was interested in what she was feeling.

Iola was sure that more than anything else that children needed security and love in their lives.

She knew now that she must not mention to

Lucy, the possibility of going away. To upset her was unkind.

"I want to stay with you," she said, "but you must not annoy your father. You must not repeat things of which you know he will disapprove."

Lucy thought this over for a moment, then she said:

"I expect because Daddy likes Aunt Isabel he wants me to be nice to her."

"Exactly!" Iola replied. "So in the future do not say anything unkind or horrid like what you said this afternoon."

"She *has* got claws!" Lucy persisted. "Her nails are long and shiny, and I'm sure if she dug them into Daddy they'd hurt!"

"That is something you must not think—and certainly must not say!" Iola said sharply.

"Shall I say I'm sorry?" Lucy asked.

She thought for a moment, then she added:

"I'm not sorry for what I said about Aunt Isabel, only sorry about Harold."

"I think it would be best to leave the whole subject alone," Iola replied.

She thought Lucy looked forlorn and she kissed her.

"Forget it," she said. "It was a silly thing to do, but we all do silly things at times."

"Have you done silly things?" Lucy enquired.

"Very silly," Iola admitted, "but I am always sorry afterwards."

"Like I am," Lucy said complacently, "and perhaps Daddy will be sorry that he likes Aunt Isabel, because it is silly of him when she has claws!"

It was hopeless, Iola thought to herself, and talking over what had happened could only make it worse.

After she had put Lucy to bed and had her supper, she went out into the garden.

She still needed her shawl but everyday since

they had been in Monte Carlo is was getting warmer, and tonight she could not feel the ice in the air from the far-away Alps as she had done before.

She had the feeling that she must enjoy every moment of what she feared in her heart would be her last days in Monte Carlo.

It was obvious that Lady Isabel intended to be rid of her, and after what had happened this afternoon she was sure that Sir Wolfe would agree that an older and more responsible Nanny would be better for Lucy.

Because Iola had grown very fond of the little girl, in fact she loved her, she found her heart aching not only for herself but for Lucy.

She prayed that she would have a Governess who would teach her in the right way, who would understand that she had an exceptional mind, and who would use methods which would help it to expand and not just stuff her memory with facts and dates.

She herself had found knowledge so fascinating that she knew she could never live long enough to absorb and assimilate all she wanted to know.

She wondered how Sir Wolfe had started on his triumphant career of accumulating a great fortune.

From the things Mr. Carter had said from time to time, she gathered that Sir Wolfe's father and mother had been ordinary, well-to-do but certainly not rich people who lived in London because Mr. Renton worked on the Stock Exchange.

Iola longed to ask somebody why they had such a brilliant son, how they had realised his capabilities, and how he had started on a career which had brought him into the company of financiers who were old enough to be his father or even grandfather.

'I wish I could talk to him about himself,' she thought.

Then she smiled as she was sure he would think it extremely impertinent if she attempted to do such a thing.

Without thinking, she walked across the lawn and was now at the same place where she had been the night that she heard the two men talking about Captain Charles Unwin.

They had been sitting on a seat in a small grove that was arranged round a little lily-pond in which there were goldfish.

In the daytime there was a magnificent view, and the flower-beds round the pool were planted with lilies which Iola loved both for their beauty and for their fragrance.

There was nobody there tonight and she walked from where she had been hidden the previous evening down some narrow steps to the seat on which the two gentlemen had been sitting.

She wanted to look at the pool in the light from the moon, which was shining silver on the sea and on the roofs of the Prince's Palace, which she could see far below her.

Almost as clearly as if they were still speaking, she could hear one of the gentlemen saying:

"We are all aware of what Isabel's like," and the other man replying: "We have all been a victim at one time or another."

A victim of what?

What did she intend to do?

One of the gentlemen had said that Charles was "up to his tricks again" and he had been asked by his friend if he intended to give Sir Wolfe "a hint."

A hint of what?

The voices seemed to echo over and over again in Iola's mind. It was as if Sir Wolfe was in danger, and yet the gentleman had said:

"If you take my advice you will let sleeping dogs lie."

"That is what I intend to do."

It was cowardly that they should not warn Sir

Wolfe of any danger he might be in, Iola told herself, if that was what it was.

Then as she thought of it, she knew that this danger was going to occur tonight.

Harold had said that Captain Charles was going away and that Lady Isabel would make the most of his absence.

Iola was very innocent. She had no knowledge of the raffish world which had been personified in the last century by the Marlborough House Set, but she was not so foolish as not to understand that gentlemen had love-affairs with married women.

She had heard her father talking about the Prince of Wales's infatuation with the beautiful Countess of Warwick, and with an actress called Lillie Langtry, of whom he fervently disapproved.

Now there was a Mrs. Keppel whose picture was always in the women's magazines and whose name appeared almost daily in the Court Circular.

Quite suddenly, like a jig-saw puzzle, everything Iola did not understand seemed to fall into place.

Of course, Sir Wolfe was having a love-affair with Lady Isabel, and the fact that her husband, Captain Charles, had gone away for the night would make it easier for them.

Sir Wolfe would kiss her. He might even go to her bedroom.

It was then that Iola sat up stiff and tense on the seat.

She could not conceive why she should have such an idea, and yet it was there and she knew, knew clearly, that Captain Charles had gone away deliberately to give Sir Wolfe the opportunity he needed to make love to his wife.

"It is horrible, wrong and wicked!" she told herself.

But why should the gentlemen who had sat where she was now sitting refer to it as "A trick" and say it annoyed them that Charles should always get away with it?

Get away with what? And what did he get out of it?

Then again another piece of the puzzle came into place.

Captain Unwin and Lady Isabel were very poor, Harold had said so, and Sir Wolfe was rich.

Just as if it were a tale she was reading in a book, Iola saw the plot unfolding in front of her eyes.

Lady Isabel, like one of the sirens or mermaids she had described to Lucy, would entice Sir Wolfe into her bedroom, and then Captain Charles would appear unexpectedly and make a scene.

There might even be a divorce, but that could no doubt be avoided if Sir Wolfe paid him to keep silent and say nothing.

"I am imagining all this," Iola told herself, and yet she was certain that something was wrong.

It was all too cleverly thought out, too well arranged, that Captain Charles should go away at this particular moment, that his wife should be alone with a man she had been flirting with obviously and possessively since the time they had left England.

"It *is* a trick! It is!" Iola told herself.

Then a warning voice told her it was nothing to do with her. One of the gentlemen had said: "If you take my advice, you will let sleeping dogs lie."

If Sir Wolfe's friends were prepared to do that, then she must do the same.

And yet she told herself that it was cowardly and whatever the outcome, it might have a bad effect on Lucy.

If Captain Charles returned and found his wife in compromising circumstances with Sir Wolfe, the servants were bound to know about it—they always knew everything.

However hard she tried to prevent them from

saying anything in front of Lucy, they would talk, and the child would be curious and perhaps ashamed.

Anyway, whatever happened it was not the type of behaviour she could connect with her father, now or ever.

Supposing, Iola reasoned, it was not a question of payment but of divorce?

If Captain Charles divorced his wife, then Sir Wolfe would in honour be obliged to marry her, and Iola could think of no woman more unfitted than Lady Isabel to be a Stepmother to Lucy.

Already Lucy disliked her because, Iola could not help thinking, she instinctively knew that Lady Isabel was shallow and vindictive, very different from what she pretended to be with her soft, sweet voice, and quite unnecessarily jealous of someone younger than herself.

'I must save Sir Wolfe!' she thought suddenly.

Without really meaning to, she rose to her feet.

'I must save him!'

It was one thing to think such a thing and quite another to know what she should do.

She walked back to the Villa.

When she reached it she was aware that it was still early in the evening and the party had not yet left for the Casino.

They invariably sat for a long time over dinner and sometimes it was nearly midnight before the carriages carried them down the hill towards the lights of Monte Carlo and the Casino, which Iola had learnt from her Guide-Book looked like a huge white wedding-cake.

She decided that one day to appease her curiosity she would drive with Lucy into Monte Carlo and look at it from the outside.

Whatever its appearance, it certainly had an allure for those who wanted to gamble, and ever since she had been at the Villa there had never been an evening when the party had not gone to the Casino.

'I shall have to warn Sir Wolfe before he leaves,' Iola thought.

She stood in the Nursery, thinking how she could possibly do such a thing. Then an idea came to her.

She went into Lucy's bedroom, and, moving very quietly so as not to disturb the little girl who was sleeping peacefully, Iola without a light searched in the darkness for a bottle that she knew stood on the wash-hand-stand.

She found it and went back to her own room.

The bottle contained some medicine which, she had been told, the Doctor had given Lucy to take when she left London.

It was a tonic, but before they reached Monte Carlo, Iola had decided it was unnecessary and the child was really better without it.

There was in consequence half of the medicine left and she tipped it away. Then with the bottle in her hand she walked along the passages to the front of the Villa.

When she reached the Hall she was aware that the ladies had left the Dining-Room but the men were still seated round the table, drinking their port and smoking cigars.

This, she knew, was the moment she wanted, as she had no wish for Lady Isabel to overhear her conversation with Sir Wolfe.

She waited until the Butler came out of the Dining-Room, then said to him:

"I wonder if you could ask Sir Wolfe to speak to me for a moment? He may think it strange, but tell him it is importnat. It concerns *Mademoiselle* Lucy."

The Butler nodded.

"I understand. Will you wait here?"

"No, tell Sir Wolfe I will be in his Study."

"I'll tell him."

The Butler went back into the Dining-Room, and Iola, holding the bottle, went into the large comfortable Study which was beside the Dining-Room.

It was a man's room, she thought, with huge leather arm-chairs, a number of book-cases from which had come the books that Harold brought her to read, and the inevitable flat-topped desk where Sir Wolfe obviously worked, even though he was on holiday.

It was piled with papers and several despatch-boxes which she thought doubtless held a number of financial secrets which Sir Wolfe's men-friends would like to peruse.

She waited for some time and she thought that perhaps Sir Wolfe, having received her message, had decided to ignore it and wait until tomorrow to hear what she had to say.

Tomorrow would be too late, she thought, and if it was, there was nothing more she could do.

Then the sound of voices and laughter that she had heard very faintly through the adjacent wall seemed to grow louder and she knew that the gentlemen were leaving the Dining-Room and were at the moment in the Hall.

A few seconds later the Study door opened and Sir Wolfe came in.

He was looking very smart in his evening-clothes and she thought his white shirt and his tail-coat became him.

It was hard to think of anything except the look of surprise in his eyes, which she felt uncomfortably were more penetrating than usual.

"You wanted to see me?" he enquired. "What about?"

"I am sorry to bother you, Sir," Iola said in what she hoped was a calm voice, although her heart was thumping, "but I find regrettably that I have run out of the tonic which I understand is important for Lucy to take every day."

"Well, what do you expect me to do about it at this time of night?" Sir Wolfe asked.

"I have made enquiries, Sir, and I understand that the Chemists in Monte Carlo are closed, but there is one that remains open all night in Nice."

"In Nice?" Sir Wolfe questioned. "You want me to send a carriage all that way? Surely it can wait until tomorrow?"

"I thought, Sir, that as the carriage would be going anyway, to collect Captain Unwin, it would not entail an extra journey, and I would like Lucy to have the medicine first thing in the morning."

"There is no carriage going to Nice tonight," Sir Wolfe replied, "and Captain Unwin will not be returning until late tomorrow or perhaps the day after."

"Oh . . . I am sorry!" Iola exclaimed. "I must have been misinformed. I understood he was definitely returning tonight."

There was silence for a moment and she thought Sir Wolfe's eyes were unpleasantly searching, and she looked down at the bottle in her hand as if she had never seen it before.

"I am . . . sorry, Sir," she said again. "I will wait until tomorrow and ask Mr. Mayhew to send to the Chemist in Monte Carlo."

She walked towards the door. Then as she reached it Sir Wolfe said:

"Wait! I want to know who told you that Captain Unwin was returning tonight."

Iola drew in her breath.

"I am afraid I . . . cannot remember . . . it must have been one of the . . . servants. They were quite . . . positive that he would be back late this evening but . . . perhaps he intends to . . . hire a carriage from Nice."

As she finished speaking she opened the door and went out.

She felt it was impossible to say or do any more.

She had done her best, and if Sir Wolfe was so obtuse that he did not understand what she was saying, or preferred to ignore what should be a warning, then whatever happened would be on his own head.

She went to her own room and undressed, but when she got into bed she could not sleep.

She kept asking herself if she had done the right thing, or if she had interfered in matters which did not concern her in the least even though she thought there might be a repercussion on her if she did so.

Then she thought that she would doubtless have to leave anyway, so what did it matter?

The only uncomfortable thing might be that if Captain Unwin did return and Sir Wolfe had not listened to what she said, he might be extremely curious as to why she should tell him one thing and Lady Isabel another.

It all seemed such a melodramatic plot and now Iola was very doubtful that her imagination had not run away with her.

She felt she would never sleep but she told herself that if she had been prepared, as Sir Wolfe's friends had been prepared, to "let sleeping dogs lie," it would have always, for the rest of her life, been heavy on her conscience.

'Besides,' she thought, and this was in fact a very fervent thought, 'why should Lady Isabel get away with it?'

Chapter Six

Wondering whether she had done the right thing, Iola as she breakfasted with Lucy could not help longing to know what had happened in the other part of the Villa.

When the footman had cleared away the dishes and she was tidying Lucy's hair, preparatory to going into the garden, Harold came into the room.

Iola was just about to say that she could not talk to him now, because she was afraid he might say something indiscreet in front of Lucy, when she saw that once again he had a present for the little girl.

This time it was a brightly coloured rubber ball and Lucy gave a cry of delight when she saw it.

Iola was quite certain he had bought it merely to give him an excuse to come into the Nursery and talk to her, but because he was so generous she felt that she could not be disagreeable and refuse to listen.

Instead she said:

"What a lovely ball! Thank Harold nicely, Lucy, then you can go and throw it on the lawn until I come and join you."

"Thank you, Harold, you are very kind," Lucy said obediently.

Holding her ball tightly in her hand, she ran

out through the French window and onto the lawn outside.

"I have told you already not to spend so much of your money," Iola said in what she tried to make a severe voice. "You must save it against a rainy day."

"A man came to the door selling them yesterday," Harold said. "I knew it'd please Miss Lucy."

It was a strange thing, Iola thought, that with all the expensive toys Lucy owned she always seemed to prefer the cheap ones which Harold brought her.

"It is very nice of you," she murmured, and knew as she spoke that Harold was bursting to relate what had happened.

She started to tidy away some of Lucy's toys and Harold began:

"Such goings-on last night! You wouldn't believe!"

Again Iola told herself she should not encourage him, but she knew that if she was honest she was extremely curious.

"When the party went off to the Casino after dinner," Harold went on, "Her Ladyship says she has a headache and wants to stay behind, and of course the Master stays with her."

He looked at Iola to see if she was following his story, then continued:

"Mr. Carter had a toothache so he leaves me on duty. I was in the Hall, waiting to help the Master into his cape and give him his tall hat, when the door of the Salon happened to be a bit open."

Iola was quite certain that Harold had been listening at it, but she said nothing and he went on, lowering his voice:

"Her Ladyship had her arm round the Master's neck, then she says ever so invitingly:

" 'I am going up to bed, darling. Do not be long. I shall be waiting for you.' "

"Oh, Harold. I do not believe you heard that," Iola protested. "you are making it up."

"Cross my heart, that's exactly what she says.

Then she comes flouncing out into the Hall and starts up the stairs."

He paused as if to make what he was saying more impressive before he went on:

"The Master followed her and she looks back and smiles at him just as if she was on the stage. Then she goes on again and he stands there watching her. Real dramatic it was!"

"It certainly sounds somewhat theatrical," Iola said drily.

"The Master goes into his Study," Harold said, "and I waits in case he wants me."

Iola repressed a smile. She was certain that Harold had waited to see if Sir Wolfe went upstairs to Lady Isabel, but she did not interrupt.

"I waits and I waits," Harold said, "for over an hour."

Iola calculated that it would now have been about one o'clock, and because she knew she had to hear the end of the story, she asked:

"What happened then?"

"I hears footsteps outside the front door," Harold replied, "and would you believe it, in walks the Captain! There hadn't been a sound of a carriage, so he must have left it at the gate, unless he walked all the way from Nice, which I'm sure he didn't!"

"It is much too far!" Iola remarked.

"He comes in very quietly," Harold went on, "and he didn't see me as I was sitting in the shadows. So he puts down his coat which he was carrying, and his hat, then he starts up the stairs. I was just wondering what I should do, when out of the Study comes the Master."

Iola gave up the pretence of doing anything else and just stood listening with her eyes on Harold.

"'Hello, Charles,' the Master says. 'I thought you were not returning until tomorrow.'

"The Captain jumps when he speaks," Harold related. "He turns round, looking ever so surprised, and there was quite a pause before he says: 'Hello, Wolfe! Not at the Casino? Where is everybody?'

" 'Isabel went to bed after dinner as she had a headache,' the Master answers, 'and I have been working.'

" 'Oh!' says the Captain."

"Is that all he said?" Iola enquired.

"That's all," Harold answered. "Then he mumbles: 'I had better go and see what is wrong with Isabel,' and he goes up the stairs in a hurry."

Iola had a feeling of relief that she had been right in warning Sir Wolfe and he had been astute enough to take what his friends would have called "a hint."

She only hoped he would not suspect that she had any ulterior motive in asking for the tonic, and that reminded her that she must cover her tracks by sending for it.

She fetched the bottle from her bedorom where she had left it.

"Would you be very kind and ask anyone who is going into Monte Carlo to get this for Miss Lucy? I think it is a well-known tonic and any reputable Chemist will have it in stock."

"I'll do that," Harold said. "But you must say, what happened last night was a bit of a 'how-d'you-do'!"

"I hope Her Ladyship's headache is better this morning," Iola said calmly, "and thank you again, Harold, for the present you gave Miss Lucy. You can see how much she enjoys playing with it."

They both looked out the window to where Lucy was bouncing the ball on the grass, then trying to catch it before it reached the ground.

"I've always been fond of children," Harold said. "I hopes when I gets married I'll have a dozen of them!"

"You had better start saving right away!" Iola laughed.

When Harold had gone she went into the garden.

She thought what Lucy needed was other children to play with, preferably brothers and sisters near her own age, but she hoped that when Sir Wolfe took another wife he would not choose anyone like Lady Isabel, although perhaps that was the type of woman he admired.

She was throwing the ball for Lucy, who was catching it quite competently, when Sir Wolfe came into the garden.

It was still early and Iola was certain there would be no sign of any of the rest of the party.

He walked across the grass towards them and Lucy cried:

"Look how clever I am at catching the ball, Daddy! See if you can catch it too."

The ball was in her hand at the moment so she threw it at him and he caught it deftly.

He threw it back but she missed the catch and ran after it as it disappeared amongst the flowering bushes on the edge of the lawn.

"Good-morning!" Sir Wolfe said to Iola.

"Good-morning, Sir."

"Lucy looks very well," he said. "You are quite certain she needs the tonic that you were in such a hurry to procure for her last night?"

"I have sent to Monte Carlo for it this morning," Iola replied. "I would not wish to disobey the Doctor's orders."

She spoke calmly, but she was uneasily aware that the colour had risen in her face, and although she did not look at him she knew that Sir Wolfe's eyes were quizzical.

"You were so concerned about her last night," he said after a moment, "that I expected to find Lucy pale and listless as she was before we came here."

Iola did not reply and after a moment he said:

"As I have told you before, I am very intuitive

when I wish to be, and I have a feeling, although it may seem a strange thing to say, that I should be grateful to you."

"Because I have made Lucy so much better, Sir?" Iola asked quickly. "I think really you should be grateful for the warm air, the sunshine, and that she is so happy here."

"By that you mean she is happy with you."

"I like to . . . think so."

Lucy came running back to them.

"I've found it!" she said. "Now throw it to me again, Daddy."

She put it into his hand and Sir Wolfe good-humouredly threw it half-a-dozen times for her before he said:

"The newspapers will have arrived by now. I must go and do some work."

He walked away without looking at her again and Iola felt her heart, which had been beating quickly, gradually slow down to normal.

'He is too clever not to know the truth,' she thought, 'but it would be very embarrassing to discuss it with him.'

That afternoon she took Lucy driving, and this time they went into Monte Carlo to look at the Casino and the harbour, which had quite a number of yachts in it besides their own.

Lucy was very excited about it and when they returned home she talked of nothing else until bedtime.

"I want to go into the Casino," she said, "I want to see the people making lots and lots of money."

"You will have to wait until you are very much older," Iola answered. "I do not think anyone is admitted until they are over twenty-one."

"It's not fair!" Lucy said. "Grown-ups have all the fun!"

"You have a different sort of fun," Iola explained,

"and they do not have exciting stories told to them like the one I am going to tell you."

"Is it very exciting, Nanny?"

"Very!" Iola replied.

"Then I'm glad I'm not grown up," Lucy said.

"I will start as soon as you are in bed and have said your prayers," Iola said.

That made Lucy undress quickly, and she said her prayers kneeling on the bed while Iola had her arms round her.

She said the prayers that she had been taught very sweetly, and when she had finished Iola kissed her.

"When you say them as nicely as that," she said, "no angel could refuse to look after you."

"You are quite sure they are there?" Lucy asked.

"Quite, quite sure," Iola replied.

"I am glad about that," Lucy said. "Now tell me your story."

She was nearly asleep by the time Iola had finished. She tucked her in, saw that the blind was drawn over the window as well as the curtains so that the light would not wake her too early, then she went into her own bedroom, which was on the other side of the Nursery.

She had a book in which she was very engrossed as it described the different regions of France and the characteristics of the people who lived in them.

Iola had a bath and put on one of the pretty lawn nightgowns that she had worn at home and read until it was quite late.

She might wear Nanny's uniform in the day, but she knew she would have been uncomfortable in the heavy calico nightgowns, almost like a tent, that Nanny had worn ever since she could remember.

It was still cold enough at night to need two blankets on the bed and as she snuggled down under them Iola thought how wonderful it was to be away from the cold winds and the snow and to know that tomorrow there would be golden sunshine, flowers, and emerald-green seas.

'I am so lucky, so very lucky!' she thought, and refused to think of her father's anger.

She was awakened by a sudden crash that made her jump, then a voice furious with anger stormed:

"What have you done with her? Tell me what you have done with her, or do I have to beat it out of you?"

Iola sat up in bed and found herself looking at Sir Wolfe, who was towering over her, his face contorted with rage, his eye-brows seeming to meet across his nose.

"What is the matter . . . what has . . . happened?" she asked.

"As if you did not know!" he shouted. "Where is Lucy? Where has she been taken?"

"What do you mean . . . where is Lucy?" Iola enquired. "She is . . . asleep."

She looked towards the communicating-door as she spoke, and realised that although it was still dark outside Sir Wolfe must have brought a lamp with him into the room.

Then she saw that the door which led to the Nursery was open, and without even thinking what she was doing, she jumped out of bed and ran just as she was, in her thin nightgown with her hair falling over her shoulders, across the Nursery and into Lucy's room on the other side.

The door was open and as she entered she saw that somebody had lit one of the gas-globes.

By the light from it she could see that Lucy's bed was empty and so was the room.

"Lucy!" she called. "Lucy, where are you? If you are hiding from me, come out at once!"

"She is not hiding here," Sir Wolfe said, "but where you have plotted to take her!"

He had followed her and Iola saw that he was

standing in the centre of the Nursery and beside him the French window which led into the garden was open.

"She must have gone into the garden," she said. "I cannot imagine why she should do such a thing."

"She has not gone into the garden," Sir Wolfe said. "She has been taken away."

"Taken . . . away?" Iola repeated stupidly.

He held out something he had in his hand. Iola saw that it was a piece of paper and took it from him.

"I found this pushed under the front door when I returned from the Casino," he said. "I am not usually so late, or I imagine it would not have been discovered until the morning."

Iola was hardly listening to him but was reading what was written on the piece of paper.

In capital lettering and written in French she read:

IF YOU WANT YOUR DAUGHTER BACK LEAVE TEN THOUSAND FRANCS UNDER THE STONE ON TOP OF THE FIRST BRIDGE ON THE ROAD TO MONTE CARLO. IF YOU TELL THE POLICE WE WILL KILL HER!

Iola read it twice as if it would not penetrate her mind. Then she cried:

"Lucy has been . . . kidnapped! Who could have . . . done such a . . . thing? How . . . could they have taken her . . . away without my being . . . aware of it?"

"That is for you to answer," Sir Wolfe said. "And do not lie and tell me you are not involved in this."

"Involved?" Iola questioned.

Now at last she realised what he had been saying to her, and for a moment she stared at him incredulously before she said:

"Do you really . . . think I could have . . . anything to do with a . . . plot to . . . kidnap Lucy? How could you . . . imagine I would hurt a . . . child I love as I love . . . Lucy?"

"You are not a very convincing liar!" Sir Wolfe retorted. "And if you know what is good for you, you will tell me the truth before the French Police force a confession out of you. Their methods, I believe, can be most unpleasant."

"Please you cannot go to the Police," Iola pleaded. "Pay the money. Let us get Lucy back."

"That is what you want, is it not?" Sir Wolfe said unpleasantly. "How can I trust you even if I paid you to bring Lucy back?"

"This has nothing to do with me!" Iola protested angrily. "You have no right whatever to think so, but I am not concerned with what you think or do not think, I am only concerned with Lucy. We have to save her . . . we have to!"

"Where is she?" Sir Wolfe demanded.

Now he took a step towards Iola and she thought for a moment he was going to strike her.

"Believe me . . . please . . . believe me," she begged. "I had . . . nothing to do . . . with this."

"I suspected you were not the Nanny you pretended to be," he said, "and looking at you now certainly confirms my suspicions."

For the first time Iola was conscious that she was wearing only a transparent lawn nightgown and instinctively her hands went to her breasts.

"Exactly!" Sir Wolfe said sarcastically. "The sort of garment you are wearing is not, I am quite sure, the usual night attire of a Nanny, and certainly too expensive to be purchased with the sort of wage you are paid."

Iola did not answer. She merely walked past him back into her own bedroom to pick up her dressing-gown which was lying on a chair by the bed.

It was even more incriminating, from Sir Wolfe's point of view, than her nightgown.

Made of white satin trimmed with lace, it had been an expensive purchase which she had been unable to resist, but for the moment all she wanted was to cover herself.

"I am not leaving here until you tell me where I can find Lucy," he said as he followed her across the Nursery.

"Will you stop being so . . . idiotic as to think I would . . . attempt to blackmail you in such . . . a cruel manner?" Iola cried. "I leave that sort of thing to your friends!"

She spoke without thinking because she was so worried and perturbed, and, seeing the anger flare into Sir Wolfe's eyes, she added quickly before he could speak:

"I am sorry. I should not have said that, and I can understand how anxious you are. But for the moment let us think only of Lucy and what is . . . happening to . . . her."

There was a little sob in Iola's voice and Sir Wolfe was silent, just watching her as she sat down on the bed and put her fingers up to her forehead as if in an effort to think.

"They must have come in from the garden," she said as if she spoke to herself. "They must have prevented her from screaming, and I suppose they could have reached the road without being seen?"

"Quite easily," Sir Wolfe agreed.

"Then where would they have gone?"

Iola was silent for a moment, then she gave a little cry.

"I know! I am almost certain I know who has done this!"

"So I am to get a confession!"

"When we were returning the day before yesterday from La Turbie," Iola said, ignoring his remarks, "there were two men. They asked me if Lucy was the daughter of 'the rich Sir Renton.' They followed us down the path to the carriage. When we left, they were talking to a man in one of those houses that are built into the rock."

She jumped off the bed as she said urgently:

"If you think they did not mean you to get this note until morning, they may have taken her there before they move her somewhere else. Quickly, get a carriage. If we hurry, we might catch them! I will be able to show you exactly where the house is."

She looked at Sir Wolfe and realised he was indecisive as to whether to trust her or not.

"Quickly! Quickly!" she said. "Every moment may be important."

"I suppose you will not slip out the window and vanish as soon as I leave the room?" he said slowly.

For a moment Iola was still. Then she said:

"You have to trust me, and after all your talk about your intuition and instinct, you should know whether I am speaking the truth or not. You should also know that I love Lucy and I would no more hurt her than cut my own throat!"

Iola spoke passionately, then Sir Wolfe's eyes met hers and she knew she had convinced him.

Without a word he turned and went from the room, and Iola pulled off her dressing-gown and started to put on the clothes she had laid ready for the morning.

They were a white cotton blouse and skirt, and as she thought she had better not look conspicuous in the darkness and perhaps also it might be cold, she snatched Nanny's serge cape from the wardrobe, then ran along the passages to the Hall.

Sir Wolfe was there and even as she reached him she heard the sound of carriage-wheels outside the door.

He was still wearing the evening-clothes in which he had come from the Casino.

A sleepy footman who was apparently on duty

put a cape over his shoulders, and without speaking Iola went ahead of him through the front door.

She saw that there was a coachman and a footman on the box, and as she was wondering if they would be enough, two grooms appeared in the drive, riding horses.

Sir Wolfe got into the carriage and as he did so, he said to the coachman:

"Go to La Turbie as quickly as you can. We will tell you where to stop."

The coachman touched his cockaded top-hat with his whip, and they were off, moving far more quickly than Iola would have expected the horses to be able to do, up such a steep incline.

"Tell me again what happened when you were at La Turbie," Sir Wolfe said.

Iola related how she had been looking at the view, then she had seen Lucy talking to two Frenchmen.

She remembered what they had said and she tried too to describe them.

"I did not notice them particularly," she said, "but they seemed to be fairly well dressed."

"Gentlemen?" Sir Wolfe asked.

Iola shook her head.

"No, but not poor and not particularly rough. Perhaps I should say they had intelligent faces."

She gave a little cry.

"They would need to be intelligent, would they not, if they were kidnappers?"

She drew in her breath.

"You do not . . . think they will be . . . unkind to Lucy?"

"We can only hope not."

"Why did you not anticipate that something like this might happen?" Iola asked frantically. "You are so rich, it is obvious people will want to extract some of it from you by one means or another."

She could not help thinking of Lady Isabel and

Captain Charles as she spoke, and she went on quickly:

"All through history people have been held for ransom. It is something that happens every day in America. Surely, because you are rich and well known, it might have occurred to you that Lucy was vulnerable?"

"In my houses in London and the country, because I have so many possessions of great value, there are always night-watchmen on duty," Sir Wolfe said, almost as if he excused himself.

"But what could be more . . . valuable than . . . Lucy?"

As if what she was thinking terrified her, she asked:

"Surely we can go quicker? The horses started off well, but now we seem to be crawling."

"It is very steep," Sir Wolfe said.

But as if he too was impatient, he let down the window and put his head out to say:

"Be as quick as you can, Gaston."

"I am doing my best, *Monsieur*," Gaston replied, "but we cannot take risks on these twisting roads at night."

Sir Wolfe sat down again.

"It will not help Lucy if we go over the edge."

"No . . . of course not," Iola agreed, "but I am frightened . . . so very . . . very frightened!"

Sir Wolfe did not answer and after a moment she said:

"I told her . . . tonight that her . . . Guardian Angel is looking after her."

"He does not appear to have been very effective," Sir Wolfe said drily.

"We cannot be certain of that as yet," Iola reflected. "After all, you said you found the letter sooner than might have been expected. What is the time?"

"About four o'clock in the morning."

"They must have left it when they took Lucy

away, believing that you would have returned from the Casino and be asleep in your bed."

"There is that possibility," Sir Wolfe conceded.

"Perhaps this is the mistake we are told criminals always make," Iola murmured. Then she added: "They may be . . . dangerous! Have you . . . anything with which to protect . . . yourself?"

"I have a revolver with me," Sir Wolfe said. "And as you have already accused me of inefficiency, let me add that it is loaded."

"I am glad," Iola said simply.

Sir Wolfe looked out the window.

"We are nearing La Turbie," he said. "What do you wish to do?"

"Tell the coachman to draw up where he did when we came here before. The house is almost opposite where we stopped."

Sir Wolfe looked out the window again and gave the directions in a low voice.

A few seconds later the horses were drawn to a standstill.

"You had better stay here," Sir Wolfe said.

"I am coming with you," Iola said firmly. "There are several houses. You would not want to go to the wrong one."

He got out of the carriage and helped her to the ground as the footman jumped down from the box.

There was only one street-lamp but it gave enough light for Iola to see the two grooms dismounting from their horses.

They tied the reins to a fence, then came to Sir Wolfe's side.

"Leave your hats by the carriage, and be ready to use your fists," he ordered.

They obeyed him and the footman did the same thing.

"Now," he said to Iola, "show me which is the house."

For one frantic moment she felt she could not be

sure. Then she pictured in her mind the two men standing talking to the Frenchman as they had driven away, and she pointed with her finger.

"That is the one," she said in a low voice. "I am sure of it!"

Sir Wolfe walked across the road followed by the grooms and footman.

They looked a formidable band, she thought, and she realised that Sir Wolfe was holding his revolver in his right hand.

She expected him to knock on the door, but she saw him say something which she could not hear to the grooms and they both took a run at the door and kicked it.

It opened with a crash, there was a woman's scream, then Iola ran across the road to see what was happening.

She had a quick glimpse of three men and a woman standing in a small, typically French kitchen, facing Sir Wolfe, obviously completely taken by surprise.

Then as Sir Wolfe began to say: "What have you done with her?" Iola heard Lucy's voice, and, pushing her way past Sir Wolfe and the men who confronted him, she went into a room that opened off the kitchen.

It was lit by a candle and Iola could see Lucy lying on a narrow bed tied down with a rope.

"Nanny! Nanny!" Lucy cried.

Then Iola's arms were round her, holding her close while tears streaked down her face.

"It is . . . all right . . . darling," she said. "It is all . . . right. We have . . . found you and you are . . . safe!"

"They carried me out of my bed," Lucy said. "I tried to scream, but a man put his hand over my mouth."

She spoke indignantly, and Iola said:

"You are safe . . . that is all that matters . . . and Daddy has . . . come to take you home."

She tried to undo the rope that held Lucy to the bed but she could not find the knot, and while she was looking for it through her tears, Sir Wolfe came into the room.

"Are you all right?" he asked Lucy.

"I want to get up, Daddy, but they've tied me down."

He found the knot and as the rope went slack Lucy flung her arms round Iola's neck.

"I knew you'd come and save me," she said. "I prayed to my Guardian Angel and he said you'd come."

"We have . . . come . . . as you . . . see," Iola answered.

"Do I get a kiss too?" Sir Wolfe enquired, and to Iola's surprise he sat down on the side of the bed.

"A big kiss!" Lucy replied. "Because you brought Nanny to save me. I guessed she'd know that I would be at La Turbie."

"She knew!"

He kissed Lucy's cheek, then stood her up on the bed.

She had one of her own blankets round her but otherwise she was only wearing the nightgown in which she had gone to bed.

"You must be frozen!" Iola exclaimed.

She started to pull off her cloak as she spoke, but Sir Wolfe with a gesture of his hand prevented her.

With Lucy's blanket still round her, he took the cloak which was still suspended from his shoulders, wrapped it round her, and picked her up in his arms.

"I think you have had enough adventuring for one night," he said. "The sooner we get you home, the better."

He walked with Lucy back into the kitchen and Iola saw now that the grooms had tied the three men's hands and feet while the woman sat weeping in a corner by the stove.

"You stay and guard these men," Sir Wolfe said, "until the Police get here. It may take a little time."

"We'll manage, Sir," one of the grooms replied with a grin. "There's not much fight in them as we took them by surprise."

Sir Wolfe handed his revolver to the eldest groom.

"I do not want you to use it," he said in a low voice, "but it will be intimidating if they put up any resistance."

"I've used one before, Sir," the groom said.

"I know that. That is why I am trusting you with it," Sir Wolfe replied.

He put both his arms round Lucy again and walked out into the street and crossed the road to the carriage.

The coachman, who had stayed with the horses, raised his hat.

"You got her, Sir! That's good news!"

"It is indeed," Sir Wolfe said. "Jacques is staying to guard our prisoners, so take us home, Gaston."

He put Lucy into the carriage and climbed in beside her. When Iola followed and sat down on the small seat opposite Lucy and her father, Sir Wolfe said:

"Sit next to Lucy. It will keep her warm."

"I'm warm now," Lucy said. "I was only cold when they brought me up here in a horrid, smelly carriage, and the men smelt of garlic."

"You have been very brave," Sir Wolfe said. "I am very proud of you."

"I was rather frightened," Lucy admitted honestly, "but then when I saw where they had brought me I was certain Nanny would remember we had seen them and they had talked to me about my windmill."

"I remembered," Iola said.

It was still difficult to speak because, although she tried to prevent it, the tears kept running from her eyes down her cheeks.

She knew it was a mixture of shock and relief, and as she thought Sir Wolfe would despise her for being so emotional, she tried to wipe them away with the back of her hand.

"I think what you want is a handkerchief," Sir Wolfe said with a faint smile.

He drew one from the pocket of his evening-coat and passed it to her over Lucy's head.

They could see each other because while they were inside the house the coachman had lit a candle-lantern which now illuminated the inside of the carriage.

It had been omitted on their outward journey as the carriage had been brought round so quickly and there had been no time to think of anything but of getting it to the front door.

Iola wiped away her tears and Lucy asked:

"Why are you crying, Nanny? I'm safe and you said I'd be safe with my Guardian Angel to watch over me."

"Yes, I know," Iola answered, "and we must both thank him very much for looking after you. But it was rather frightening for your father and me when we found you had gone."

"It was very wicked of them to steal me away," Lucy said. "Will they go to prison for years and years?"

"I hope so," Sir Wolfe answered, "and I promise you it is something that will never happen again in the future. There will always be guards on duty round the Villa and anywhere else that we live."

"Guards?" Lucy asked with interest. "Will they be soldiers?"

"I am afraid I am not important enough for that," Sir Wolfe smiled, "but they will be men trained to keep away kidnappers, burglars, and criminals of every sort."

"That'll be exciting!" Lucy said. "And Nanny'll be able to make up a story about this adventure, won't you, Nanny?"

"Perhaps," Iola answered, "but it is not a story I want to think about or tell at the moment."

"I will tell a story about a brave little girl called Lucy," Sir Wolfe said.

"Was she kidnapped?" Lucy asked.

"Yes."

"And she was saved?"

"Yes, she was so sensible and brave about it that she was given a medal."

Lucy gave a cry of delight.

"Is that what I'll get?"

"You will have to wait and see, but I have a feeling that tomorrow you will receive a very important gold medal."

"That'll be exciting!" Lucy said. "I shall wear it always, always, and tell people why I won it."

Iola was looking at Sir Wolfe in surprise.

She had never expected him to be so imaginative or to say exactly the right thing to take away Lucy's fears.

She was well aware that most children and certainly any of the women of his acquaintance would be having hysterics after what they had been through. But Lucy was behaving just, Iola thought, as he would want her to, and she was glad he appreciated the fact.

They reached the Villa, and by this time the sky was lightening a little and the stars were growing fainter.

On the door-step was waiting Mr. Mayhew, together with the Butler, Carter, Harold, and most of the French servants.

The carriage came to a standstill and Mr. Mayhew came to the door.

"You have found her—thank God! When I learnt what had happened, I couldn't believe that anything so terrible could occur to Lucy."

"I'm safe!" Lucy replied before anyone else could speak. "I'm to have a medal—a gold medal—for being so brave!"

Sir Wolfe got out of the carriage first and lifted Lucy into his arms.

"All's well that ends well, Mayhew," he said, "but this is something which must not happen again."

"I should hope not," Mr. Mayhew said.

Iola thought he looked white and shaken and that all the other servants, especially Carter and Harold, had an anxious expression in their eyes despite the fact that they were smiling because Lucy was safe.

"I think what Lucy and Miss Dawes require at the moment is something hot to drink," Sir Wolfe said as he walked through the front door.

"Yes, of course," Mr. Mayhew said. "I'll see to it."

He gave the orders to the Butler and Sir Wolfe walked on down the passage which led to the Nursery.

The gas-lamps had all been lit since they had been away, and through the open door of her bedroom Iola could see her lace-trimmed dressing-gown and nightgown lying on the bed.

She blushed, then told herself that it did not matter.

Sir Wolfe had seen them now, and although he would no longer think she was a kidnapper, he would certainly be convinced more than he was already that she was no ordinary Nanny.

He had sat down in an arm-chair with Lucy on his knees and surprisingly gently he was taking his cape from her shoulders while keeping her wrapped in the blanket which had been on her bed.

Looking at him as he listened to Lucy chattering away about her medal, Iola thought he was very different from the man who had raged at her so violently when she had awakened to find herself denounced as a kidnapper.

Then as she stood looking at him, he looked up at her and she felt as their eyes met that her heart turned several somersaults.

It was suddenly very difficult to breathe.

Chapter Seven

Iola slipped out of bed very quietly so as not to disturb Lucy.

She realised by the golden light coming from between the curtains that it was very late in the morning, and surprisingly, after all that had happened, she had slept well, although she had found it hard at first to go to sleep.

This was because her heart was thumping and she was aware of strange sensations she had never known, but, although she tried to pretend otherwise, it was easy to put a name to them.

After Sir Wolfe had held Lucy on his knees for a few minutes he had said:

"You must go to bed, my dearest, and I must send for the police."

Lucy, with her head against his shoulder, was almost asleep, and holding her in his arms he rose to his feet, but when he would have carried her into her own bedroom she gave a little cry.

"Perhaps they'll come back and take me away again."

"She can sleep with me," Iola interposed.

"Of course," Sir Wolfe agreed. "I will fetch a footman to move her bed."

"There is no need for that," Iola said. "There is

not much of the night left, and my bed is big enough for two."

Lucy roused herself to say:

"Do you mean I can sleep with you, Nanny? I'd like that, I'd like it very much!"

"You must remember," Sir Wolfe said as he carried her into Iola's room, "that you are both to go to sleep and not talk. I do not want to look at two haggard young women tomorrow!"

"We'll go to sleep at once," Lucy promised, "but it'll be exciting to sleep with Nanny."

Sir Wolfe laid her down in Iola's bed and pulled the blankets over her.

Then as he straightened himself he looked at Iola. Their eyes met and once again there was that strange vibration between them.

She tried to turn away, but it was impossible. She felt as if he captured her and held her prisoner.

Then after a moment he said in a low voice that was unexpectedly deep:

"Good-night and thank you."

She could not answer him, and then he had gone from the room, shutting the door quietly behind him.

Only when she undressed and got into bed beside Lucy, who was already fast asleep, did she realise that something had happened to her that had never happened before in her whole life.

She was in love!

'It is not possible!' she thought now. 'I must have imagined it.'

As she picked up her clothes and moved very quietly out of her own room and across the Nursery into Lucy's, she knew that her heart was dancing with the sunshine she could see through the uncurtained windows.

The flowers in the garden and the water-fountain pouring iridescent like a thousand tiny rainbows seemed to be part of a joy which was irrepressible and a glory which seemed to encompass her.

Then as she dressed herself in the clean white blouse and stiff cotton skirt, and clasped Nanny's silver-buckled belt round her small waist, she told herself that she was crazy and the sooner she faced facts the better.

To Sir Wolfe she was a servant, one who was engaged to look after his daughter.

If he had the slightest suspicion that her feelings for him were anything but respectful, he would consider it an impertinence and she would doubtless be dismissed immediately.

As if the thought jerked her mind back to what had happened already, her elation died within her, as she remembered what he had said when he accused her of kidnapping Lucy.

"I suspected you were not the Nanny you pretended to be!" he had stormed. "And looking at you now certainly confirms my suspicions."

She had forgotten that, she thought, in all that had happened. But today he would want an explanation.

She put up her hands to her face in an effort to think.

If she told him the truth, then it was obvious he would not want her to go on pretending to be a Nanny. He would know too that the real Nanny Dawes was dead and there was no chance of her ever coming to look after Lucy.

But she knew it would be almost impossible to lie to him, to make up some story that he would believe when his penetrating eyes were looking into her and seeking the truth.

"What can I do? What can I do?"

She felt the question turning over and over in her mind, and all the time every nerve in her body was protesting against leaving him and leaving Lucy and being alone in a strange and frightening world.

But what else could she do?

Go home and marry Lord Stoneham, if he would still have her? Or try and find herself employment of some sort?

The idea was terrifying, even if Sir Wolfe was generous enough to assist her.

Then she told herself perhaps he would accept her as what she had first planned to be—a Nursery-Governess.

'I could stay and teach Lucy,' she thought, 'and . . . see him.'

That, she knew, was what she really wanted: to see him, to be near him, to know that he existed in her world, whatever he might be doing, however indifferent he might be to her as a woman.

Yet perhaps he had not been indifferent last night, when his eyes had held hers captive.

But she was not sure.

She was so inexperienced where men were concerned.

Maybe because they had been through a terrifying, dramatic experience together, just for one moment they had been linked by their anxiety, followed by relief?

Now they would go back to normal, and Sir Wolfe would again be reserved and indifferent and doubtless contemptuous of the fanciful ideas she had taught Lucy.

'He would never tolerate a Governess,' Iola thought despairingly, 'who told his daughter about mermaids and Guardian Angels.'

She gave a deep sigh and walked to the window to stand breathing in the warm air, feeling it like a caress against the softness of her skin.

'I thought love would be like sunshine,' she thought, 'warm, gentle, and a joy. But what I am feeling is agonising, knowing I may lose the small contact I have with the man I love.'

Then she told herself that she was being ridiculous in every way to love somebody like Sir Wolfe.

His world was one she could not enter even as her father's daughter, because she was so young, so unsophisticated, and so ignorant of everything that was connected with his way of life.

His world was filled with Royalty, luxury, finance, beautiful women, and there was no place there for her.

She thought of Lady Isabel and knew that she was the type, apart, of course, from her perfidy, that Sir Wolfe would like.

She imagined that her conversation would be witty and stimulating in addition to a sugar-sweetness in her voice that was enticing and seductive.

"How can I compete with that?" Iola asked herself hopelessly.

Then she gave a bitter little laugh.

It was not even a question of "competing," for she would not have the opportunity to do so.

She was just a servant who had been engaged to perform certain services and would doubtless be dismissed as not being very satisfactory.

Iola felt at that moment as if she went down into a special little hell of loneliness and despair which was all her own.

Then she told herself that whatever her personal feelings might be, the world in which Lucy lived must go on.

She rang the bell and when the footman came she asked him the time.

"It's just after midday," he replied.

"Then Miss Lucy and I will have to combine breakfast with luncheon," Iola said. "There is no hurry, she is not yet awake."

"The Master said when you woke, he'd like to see you in the Study."

Iola's heart gave a little leap and she felt two emotions at once: joy and apprehension.

"I will go to him now," she said, "but please ask one of the maids to sit in the Nursery until I return in case Miss Lucy wakes up."

"I will tell them right away, *M'mselle*," the footman replied.

Iola ran to the mantelpiece over which hung a mirror.

She looked at herself, wondering if because of what she now felt within her she would appear any different.

But her face seemed much the same except that her eyes were very large and a little frightened.

Instinctively she put up her hands to her hair to smooth it into place.

Ever since she had been in Monte Carlo it had been impossible to pull it back severely as she had tried to do when she first came.

It was too buoyant, too full of life, and although she still pinned it tightly into a bun at the nape of her neck, it rose in a wave above her forehead and she looked like a sketch by Charles Dana Gibson of the beautiful American women who had introduced a new fashion to the Social World.

"What will he say to me? What will he want to know?" Iola asked her reflection.

Though her lips moved there was no answer in the darkness of her eyes.

Feeling as if every footstep was an effort, she moved along the corridors which led to the Study, and when she reached the door she found it impossible to go in, impossible to face Sir Wolfe.

There was so much to be explained, so much at stake, and he would be angry because he had been deceived.

She remembered his obsession that Lucy must tell the truth, and she knew it was because he himself loathed lies and hated everything that was not straightforward and above-board.

"Perhaps I should . . . run away before he . . . hates

me for what I . . . am," Iola told herself miserably.

Then a pride that perhaps came from her ancestors, many of whom had been soldiers like her father, came to her assistance.

She put up her small chin and resolutely opened the door and walked into the Study.

Sir Wolfe was sitting at his desk, a pile of papers in front of him.

As he looked up and saw her, Iola found it impossible to meet his eyes, and she could only stand trembling a little, waiting for him to tell her what to do.

"You are rested?"

Somehow it was not what she had expected him to say and she felt herself stammering as she replied:

"Y-yes . . . thank you . . . but Lucy is . . . still asleep."

"That makes it easier for us to talk. Shall we sit down?"

She thought she would be expected to sit in the chair which stood in front of his desk, but he had risen to his feet and now he indicated a sofa and chairs which stood on the other side of the room and were arranged so that one had a view of the garden and, beyond, the exquisite coastline and sea.

Iola forced herself to walk to the sofa, and when she sat down on it she felt as if her legs would have carried her no farther.

She clasped her fingers together in an effort to prevent herself from trembling and turned her face away from Sir Wolfe's to look out into the garden.

He stood staring at her for a moment, the sunshine turning her hair to gold. Then he sat down on the chair which faced her and said quietly:

"Well, are you going to tell me?"

"Tell you . . . what?"

"About yourself. I have been wondering, as you can imagine, what your secret can be."

Iola drew in her breath. Then she said:

"Could we not . . . leave things as they . . . are? You know that Lucy is . . . happy with me, and that I . . . love her. Is that not . . . enough?"

"You would think me very inhuman," Sir Wolfe remarked, "if I was completely without curiosity."

"You know at . . . least that I was not . . . guilty of what you . . . suspected."

Because it suddenly struck her how incredible it was that he should think such things of her, that he should imagine for one moment she would hurt Lucy in any way, her hesitation vanished and she asked almost angrily:

"How could you think . . . how could you imagine for . . . one moment that I would do . . . such a thing?"

She looked at him as she spoke. Then the expression in his eyes made her shy and she felt the little burst of anger, which had made her speak as she had, die away.

"Considering that you found Lucy and behaved so bravely in doing so," Sir Wolfe said, "I am of course prepared to apologise. Will you forgive me?"

There was a note in his voice that sounded like music, and Iola answered quickly:

"Yes . . . of course! I suppose I can . . . understand that the . . . shock of knowing she had been kidnapped made you . . . suspect everybody."

"Especially you!"

"Why me?"

"Because you are quite obviously not the Nanny you pretend to be. You are too intelligent, the wrong class, and, of course, far too beautiful!"

Iola's eyes widened for a moment, then the colour swept up her face in a rosy glow.

"Much too beautiful!" Sir Wolfe repeated. "And I find it impossible to guess why, looking as you do, you should choose to disguise yourself as you have, and in my house."

Iola's fingers tightened and she could not speak. After a moment he said:

"I imagine you are hiding—but from whom? And why?"

"Y-yes . . . I am . . . hiding."

Her voice was barely above a whisper and he said:

"What have you done? Looking at you, I cannot believe it is anything criminal."

"You were prepared to . . . think so . . . last night."

He smiled.

"We are duelling with words, and I suggest we start at the beginning. Do you realise I do not even know your name? What is it?"

As if the word was dragged from her she replied:

"Iola."

"It is a pretty name, and it suits you, but what else?"

She was about to reply that she had no intention of telling him, but she thought it was not likely to mean anything to him.

"Herne."

She felt without looking at him that Sir Wolfe wrinkled his forehead in an effort at concentration before he asked:

"What happened to the real Nanny Dawes? The one who was engaged by Mayhew."

"She . . . she . . . died."

There was no mistaking the little throb in Iola's voice and Sir Wolfe said:

"That would account for the stricken look in your eyes. I presume she had been your Nanny when you were a child?"

Iola nodded.

For the moment it was impossible to speak for fear she might burst into tears.

"So Nanny Dawes died and you decided to take her place," Sir Wolfe said. "But why? Why?"

Perhaps because his voice was quiet and sympathetic, Iola was able to say:

"I had gone to Nanny for help and advice . . . she

told me she had this new position with you and she was very . . . excited about it. She was looking forward to . . . going on a yacht for the first time. She thought it would be . . . like a . . . travelling house."

Iola's voice was almost incoherent as she went on:

"I . . . I stayed the . . . night with her in her . . . cottage. In the . . . morning I f-found that she was . . . d-dead!"

Her voice broke and although she tried to check them, the tears overflowed and ran down her cheeks.

Sir Wolfe looked at her for a long moment, then he rose from the chair in which he was sitting.

"I think that once again," he said quietly, "you need my handkerchief."

He put one into Iola's hand and sat down beside her on the sofa.

"I can understand what you felt," he said, "and I think too I can understand why you thought you could look after Lucy as your Nanny had looked after you."

"I tried," Iola said, "and you know I have made her . . . happy . . . as I was when . . . Nanny was with me."

Her voice was indistinct because she was holding the handkerchief to her eyes, and after a moment Sir Wolfe said:

"Stop crying, my darling, and tell me why you ran away."

For a moment Iola thought that she could not have heard him aright and that she was dreaming. She turned her face up to his, staring at him, the tears wet on her long eye-lashes.

He was smiling and there was an expression in his eyes that she had never seen before.

"Wh-what did you . . . say?" she whispered.

"I think you heard me."

He put his arm round her as he spoke and drew

her gently against him, and she felt a streak of excitement like a shaft of lightning run through her.

Then because it was so intense she hid her face against his shoulder.

His arms were very strong and comforting and after a moment he said:

"You had intrigued and enchanted me before last night, but when I thought you had deceived me and were instrumental in kidnapping Lucy, the agony I suffered told me that what I felt was not the ordinary rage of a man who has been let down, but one who has been disillusioned by—love."

"H-how could you . . . love me?" Iola asked childishly.

Sir Wolfe smiled. Then he put the fingers of his free hand under her chin and turned her face up to his.

"There are a great many answers I could give to that question," he said, "but the real truth is that what I feel for you is something I have never felt before in my whole life. Because I know that whoever you may be, whatever you have done, or whatever you are hiding, is unimportant, then what I am feeling must be love."

"Are you . . . sure? Really sure?" Iola asked. "I knew this . . . morning that . . ."

She suddenly felt she could not say what she herself felt. Her voice died away and her eye-lashes fluttered and lay against her cheeks.

"What did you feel this morning?" Sir Wolfe asked.

"I do not . . . think I can . . . tell you."

"Shall I make it easier?"

His lips were on hers.

Iola had never been kissed, and even though she had admitted to herself that she loved Sir Wolfe, she had not expected that his lips would not only feel as if they took possession of her but would also give her an ecstasy that she had no idea existed.

For a moment there was just the rapture of knowing that his arms were holding her and his mouth was on hers.

Then the lightning she had felt before, but more intense, more startling, swept through her like a streak of burning flame.

It seemed to ignite her whole body so that his lips took into his keeping her heart, her soul, everything that was hers, and made it a part of himself.

The room vanished, the whole world in which they lived. There was only a boundless sky and a light that seemed as it enveloped them to be a part of God and his angels.

It was so perfect, so wonderful, that Iola felt as if she must have died and was in a Heaven where there were no more problems, difficulties, or fears, only love.

It might have been a few minutes or a century of time before Sir Wolfe raised his head to look down at her shining eyes, her flushed cheeks, and her softly parted lips.

"Now tell me the truth," he said, and his voice was deep and a little unsteady.

"I . . . love you! I . . . love . . . you!"

She felt as if the words were accompanied by the music from some celestial choir.

"That is what I want you to say," Sir Wolfe replied, "and, my darling heart, was there ever anyone so sweet, so innocent, so untouched?"

His lips twisted into a smile as he said:

"Last night after you had perplexed and bewildered me, I tortured myself with wondering if you were married or were hiding from some man. But I know now you have never been kissed."

He paused, then he said:

"That is true, is it not?"

"I . . . I had no idea a . . . kiss could be so . . . wonderful!" Iola said. "No-one has ever . . . tried to kiss me . . . until now."

"That is what I thought!" Sir Wolfe replied. "I could not believe that you were anything but pure and perfect, as you appear to be."

Iola drew in her breath.

"I . . . must tell you . . . why I am . . . running away."

She knew, because his arm tightened a little, that he was afraid of what he might hear.

"My father . . . who is a General. . . and very overpowering . . . wants me to . . . marry somebody called . . . Lord Stoneham."

Because she had not wanted to tell him, Iola hid her face against his shoulder.

"Stoneham?" Sir Wolfe repeated. "I seem to know the name. You cannot mean Lord Stoneham who is one of the Lords-in-Waiting to the King, and who I believe is Lord Lieutenant of some County. He's an old man!"

"Yes . . . that is . . . he."

"How could you marry a man old enough to . . ." Sir Wolfe began. Then he stopped.

"Perhaps I also am too old for you."

"No . . . no!" Iola cried. "I love you! It would not matter what age you were. But Lord Stoneham is horrid! He is a friend of Papa's and I was told I had to marry him . . . so . . . I ran away."

Sir Wolfe's arms held her closer still.

"Thank God you did something so sensible! Supposing I had not met you until after you were married? Supposing I had known then, as I know now, that you are the only woman I have ever wanted as my wife?"

He would have said more, but he knew instinctively that Iola was thinking of the woman to whom he had once been married.

She did not speak, but after a moment he said:

"We have so much explaining to do to each other, but somehow it is really unimportant because we know the only thing that really matters is that I love you and you love me."

"The only . . . thing," Iola whispered.

"But I suppose what must be said must be said," Sir Wolfe went on. "So I will tell you that I married a woman whom I admired and who seemed eminently suitable in every way, believing, as if it were a business deal, that it was to the advantage of us both."

He sighed and went on:

"I thought—absurdly, as I now know—that I would never know the kind of ecstatic love extolled by the poets, which I was certain was not an emotion to be indulged in by any sensible man."

"And . . . now?" Iola interrupted breathlessly.

Sir Wolfe looked down at her and smiled.

"I know the poets were right and what I feel is as romantic and lovely as the fairies which you told Lucy about in secret, the mermaids that you and she think swim in the sea, and the angels which kept her company last night and saved her from the kidnappers."

Iola gave a little cry of sheer happiness.

"How can you say such wonderful things?" she asked.

Now the tears were back in her eyes.

"You were right and I was wrong," Sir Wolfe said, "and I know now that such things are all part of love, the love you have given my daughter and the love that I believe you have for me."

It was a question.

"I love you so much," Iola answered, "it is impossible to . . . express it in words. So please . . . will you . . . kiss me . . . again?"

He pulled her almost roughly to him and kissed her until she felt as if she were disembodied and no longer human.

Then as he took his lips from hers he said:

"I love you—God knows why I have had to wait until now to learn that love is the only thing worth fighting or struggling for."

"It is . . . wonderful . . . wonderful!"

"And so are you, my lovely one."

Iola's face was so radiant with happiness that more gently he kissed the softness of her cheeks, her eyes, and her small chin.

Then he kissed each of her ears and his lips found a little pulse beating in her neck above the high collar of Nanny's white blouse.

It gave Iola a strange sensation she had not known before, so intense it was half a wild pleasure, half a pain, and as her breath came quickly in little gasps, Sir Wolfe said:

"My darling, my sweet—I will be very gentle with you—I will not frighten you."

"You do . . . not frighten me . . ." Iola whispered, "but you make me . . . feel very strange. . . ."

"What do you feel?"

"Very, very excited and sort of . . . wild."

"My adorable, precious little love!"

Sir Wolfe's voice was very deep and passionate. Then because she suddenly felt shy, Iola said a little breathlessly:

"You must . . . finish your . . . story."

"I am trying to," Sir Wolfe replied, "but it is difficult when you say such things to me. Oh, my precious, I cannot think what has happened, but you have changed my whole life and I am not the same man I was."

"I want you . . . just as you . . . are."

"And I want you," he said, "in a thousand ways which I will tell you about later."

"Finish . . . your story," Iola begged.

She knew that whatever he told her was unimportant. He had said all that really mattered—that he wanted her.

"It was only after I was married," Sir Wolfe began, and she knew that he forced himself to continue, "that I discovered my wife was a habitual liar and was in fact indifferent to me as a man. When Lucy was on the way she made it clear how much I bored her, and how even more boring, as far as she was concerned, it was having a baby."

His voice sharpened a little as he said:

"Yet she could not be frank with me even over that, but lied about everything so inadequately that any man, however stupid, would have known she was not speaking the truth."

Iola gave a little sigh.

"Now I understand why you want Lucy always to hear the truth... but there are... different sorts of ... truths."

"I know that now," Sir Wolfe said with a smile. "You must teach me, as you have taught Lucy, to use my imagination and to believe not only with my brain but with my instinct."

Iola gave a cry of delight.

"That expresses exactly what I want to say. You are so clever, so perceptive, but..."

She stopped, looking up at him apprehensively until he asked:

"But what? Tell me the end of the sentence."

"I am... afraid that you will find me so... unsophisticated and so... ignorant about so many things that I shall... bore you."

"Do you really think that is possible? I can imagine nothing more exciting than to teach you what you do not know already. If it is about love, my darling one, then I shall be a very exacting teacher."

"Are you ... sure you do not ... want me to be like the... other women who have... interested you?"

Iola was thinking again of the beauty of Lady

Isabel, her elegance and the impression she gave of being so assured and worldly-wise.

"I want you just as you are!" Sir Wolfe said fiercely. "I am entranced by your beauty, your quick little brain, and I adore you when you look frightened and unsure of yourself."

"That is what I want you to say," Iola answered. "And if you will teach me to be . . . exactly as you want me to be . . . perhaps I shall be able to make you . . . happy."

"There is no doubt about that," Sir Wolfe replied, "and so, my darling, there only remains one thing to decide—how soon will you marry me?"

"Can we be married?" Iola asked. "I am only eighteen, and I shall have to have my father's consent."

"I have a feeling it will not be difficult to get round that problem if we are married here in Monte Carlo," he said. "Once you are my wife, I think there will be little your father can do about it. In any case, without being conceited, I doubt if he will make many objections."

Iola was sure that was true. She felt as if Sir Wolfe had solved her last problem and there were no more difficulties and everything was golden with sunshine.

Because she felt her love welling up in her almost like a wave in the sea, she whispered:

"Please . . . can we be married very . . . quickly? I want to belong to you and be quite . . . quite sure this is not a wonderful dream from which I shall . . . wake up."

"I feel the same," Sir Wolfe said, "we will be married at the very latest tomorrow. I will send Mayhew into Monte Carlo immediately."

Iola moved from his arms to stand up.

As he rose too, she looked at him, thinking that no man could be more attractive.

She felt a sudden panic run through her as if everything they had said and done was, as she had been afraid, part of a dream.

It could not be true. She could not be fortunate enough to become the wife of this brilliant, exciting man.

Because she was afraid, she turned instinctively to him, holding on to him, her head thrown back because he was so much taller than she was, to look up at him and say beseechingly:

"It is true... tell me it is true... make me... believe that you really... love me."

"I will do that, my precious little love," he answered, "and once we are married you will never doubt it again."

He pulled her close against him but he kissed her very gently and tenderly in a way that made her feel as if he gave her a gift so precious, so valuable, that it was spiritually a sacrament.

Then he said:

"Go now and change your uniform, in which you look adorable, but which is no longer necessary, into something more feminine. I want to see you as you really are, and I am certain everything you possess will be as alluring and perhaps as provocative as the nightgown you wore last night."

Iola blushed and hid her face.

"I feel... ashamed that you should have... seen me like that."

"Angry though I was," Sir Wolfe said, "I thought no-one could be so lovely, so absolutely exquisite. It is going to be hard, my beautiful one, to wait until we are married before I can see you again with your hair falling over your shoulders, your perfect body showing through the thin lawn."

"Y-you are... making me very... embarrassed."

"I am not going to tell you what you make me feel when I think of you like that," Sir Wolfe said. "All

I will say, my sweet, is that no fairy or mermaid you have ever imagined could be so alluring."

He bent his head and kissed her hair. Then he said:

"Go away! You are making me far too poetical—positively lyrical! I am beginning to be afraid that even my fortune will turn out to be fairy-gold and disappear at the touch of your hands."

"If you lost everything you possess," Iola said, "I should still love you... not only as much as I do now, but perhaps... more, because then I might be of some... use to you."

There was a passionate note in her voice which Sir Wolfe did not miss.

"I adore you for saying that," he said. "At the same time, you have already been of use to me, my darling, and your usefulness in the future will be so boundless that I cannot now describe it in words. But when I teach you as I intend to do about love, you will understand how much you mean to me."

He put his arms round her again and Iola thought he was going to kiss her, but before he could do so, she said:

"I think... Lucy should have brothers and sisters to... play with... and if I could give you a son... I would feel I was very... useful."

"I knew last night," Sir Wolfe replied, "when I saw you in that squalid house, holding Lucy in your arms with the tears running down your cheeks, that I would give everything I possessed to have a child by you."

Now his lips were on hers, passionate and compelling, fierce and demanding. But as Iola felt herself pulsating in his arms and her heart was beating as wildly as his, she knew she was not afraid.

This was the fire of love, the fire that seemed to burn through her and which she knew was ignited from the fire in him.

She did not understand, but she felt as if she wanted to be closer and still closer to him, to burn even more fiercely until she was beyond thought, beyond everything but the ecstasy he evoked in her.

Then when she felt as if it was impossible to feel any more and not to die from the wonder of it, he set her free.

"Go and do as I told you," he said, and his voice was hoarse, "and let me arrange our marriage. I am so much in love that every hour you are not mine will seem like a thousand years."

Iola felt too bemused by his kisses to begin to understand what he was saying.

She only waited to press her lips passionately against his shoulder, then because he commanded it she turned and ran from the room, speeding down the passage until she reached the Nursery.

As she entered it, she heard Lucy call her.

"Nanny, is that you?"

She ran into her bedroom to see Lucy sitting up in bed.

"I'm awake, and I'm home!" Lucy cried. "Isn't that wonderful?"

Then as she looked at Iola, at the radiance which had transformed her face, at the breath coming quickly from between her lips, she exclaimed:

"You look different! Oh, Nanny, what's happened to you? What is it?"

Iola walked towards her.

"It is only love, dearest," she answered with a lilt in her voice, "only love!"

ABOUT THE AUTHOR

BARBARA CARTLAND, the world's most famous romantic novelist, who is also an historian, playwright, lecturer, political speaker and television personality, has now written over 200 books.

She has also had many historical works published and has written four autobiographies as well as the biographies of her mother and that of her brother Ronald Cartland, who was the first Member of Parliament to be killed in the last war. This book has a preface by Sir Winston Churchill.

Barbara Cartland has sold 100 million books over the world, more than half of these in the U.S.A. She broke the world record in 1975 by writing twenty books, and her own record in 1976 with twenty-one. In addition, her album of love songs has just been published, sung with the Royal Philharmonic Orchestra.

In private life, Barbara Cartland, who is a Dame of the Order of St. John of Jerusalem, has fought for better conditions and salaries for Midwives and Nurses. As President of the Royal College of Midwives (Hertfordshire Branch), she has been invested with the first Badge of Office ever given in Great Britain which was subscribed to by the Midwives themselves. She has also championed the cause for old people and founded the first Romany Gypsy Camp in the world.

Barbara Cartland is deeply interested in Vitamin Therapy and is President of the British National Association for Health.